THE DEATH OF THE BODY

C. K. STEAD was Professor of English at the University of Auckland for 20 years until 1986. He is known among students of literature as the author of *The New Poetic*, a study of Yeats, Eliot and the Georgian poets. He has written eight novels and has published ten volumes of poetry and two volumes of short stories. He is the only author to have won the New Zealand Book Award for both poetry and fiction, winning twice for his novels *All Visitors Ashore* and *The Singing Whakapapa*. In 1984 he was awarded the C.B.E. for services to New Zealand literature and he is a Fellow of the Royal Society of Literature. His latest novel, *Talking about O'Dwyer*, will be published by Harvill in 2000.

T0316147

C. K. Stead

THE DEATH OF
THE BODY

THE HARVILL PRESS

LONDON

First published by Harvill in 1986

This edition first published in Great Britain in 1999 by
The Harvill Press
2 Aztec Row, Berners Road
London N1 0PW

1 3 5 7 9 8 6 4 2

A CIP catalogue record is available
from the British Library

ISBN 1 86046 754 7

Designed and typeset in Lintron Bembo by
Wyvern Typesetting Limited, Bristol

Printed and bound in Great Britain by Clays Ltd, St Ives PLC

TO
CAROL O'BRIEN

ONE

To Begin with My Room in London

It looks over a square. It's already late autumn and the leaves are showering down and heaping over lawns and paths. Those remaining are still a curious mixture of green and brown. The afternoon light slants through them, revealing the pattern of boughs that has been concealed.

I introduce myself by looking out. I introduce myself only to dismiss myself as of no consequence. I'm a travelling salesman, an itinerant bard, a newsman in search of a happy ending. I'm the life-and-soul of the party-of-one. I'm the voice of the Story.

The Story is the blue folder lying on my bed under the Matisse poster put up to brighten my room. As yet there's nothing in the folder, but it speaks to me. I'm under instruction. If you don't like explanations to be fanciful you can believe, if you prefer, that what I call the Story is something in my head. A kind of instinct. Whatever it is, it's commanding, dictatorial, hectoring, and inclined to sulk when it doesn't get its own way. I'm a slave to it, as you will see.

Am I a Londoner? No. Do I come from the other end of the earth? Yes. Have I name? To be honest I have not. I am, as I've told you, the voice of the Story. But if you don't believe a voice can exist without a name, call me Ishmael, or Philip, or take whatever name you find on the cover of the book. These won't be correct, but if they silence your anxieties and permit you to listen, then let them serve. In the end an identity will be forged. Or it won't. That will be for you to decide.

Soon I will be leaving London for Milan. This room will be kept for me while I'm away, and I will return to it before we are finished. Why Milan? That too will be revealed, to me as to you. Or perhaps it will never be clear why Milan. I am under orders and you will travel with me.

Meanwhile my task is to put before you, by way of prologue, a single scene, a single action. To it too we will return.

So imagine a kitchen – a modern kitchen, quite well equipped, and with a machine on the sink bench for grinding carrots to make carrot juice. It's not a London kitchen. You can see that by looking through the windows. It's in a suburb somewhere in what's called the New World – lots of space and vegetation and other modern kitchens angled this way and that looking out and looking in at one another. Sun-decks, plantains, bamboo and papyrus. Even a cabbage tree and, up the bank there, a pohutukawa to tell you this is New Zealand. We New Zealanders have, you see, lived through and left behind the anguish and the nostalgia of our colonial transplantation. Now it's no longer English plants we put in our gardens. In the north, anyway, where it's warm, we grow things that suggest we live in the tropics, which is not the case.

Out in the drive that runs up to the big modern house next door a car has pulled up and a tall man is getting out. All this can be seen from our kitchen, and is being watched by three men, two in their early forties, one in his twenties. The younger one is leaning along the top of the refrigerator, trying to focus a camera with a long lens on

2

the man getting out of the car. He's having difficulty because one of the other men, wearing a grey shirt with darker grey stripes, is standing at the window, obstructing his line of vision.

The third man, seated at the kitchen table and looking out into the drive from another window, says "Get him, Jack-boy."

The young man with the camera says "I can't. The prof's in the way."

And then, as the third man turns from his window and looks to see what's happening in the kitchen, the young man with the camera says impatiently "Out of the way Prof. Quick. For Christ's sake I'll miss the bugger."

But the "prof" who is causing the obstruction is suddenly angry. Even as the sound of the camera shutter can be heard, once, twice, a third time, a fourth, he begins to speak very coldly and firmly to the other two. He tells them this is his kitchen – his and his family's – and he's had enough of them cluttering it up and behaving as if they owned the place. More than enough. He's asking them to leave. Not next week. Not tomorrow. Now.

And there's the silence of an angry deadlock.

My room in London. A kitchen in Auckland.

My London room contains the blue folder. Now the blue folder contains the Auckland kitchen. These are my instructions. Follow me as I follow them, and we should in due course get back where we began.

TWO

The Word of the Body

This is a story about three men and four women, drugs, and a dead body. That's one way of describing it. Another, less exciting, would be to say it's about the problem of Body and Mind, or body-and-mind, or body versus mind. When you take the word body like that and make it a problem in philosophy it goes dead on you in a different way. I can't avoid that. One of my three men is a professor of philosophy and his wife has become a Sufi. The strain caused by this divergence of paths will be revealed. And however remote from one another they may seem, the professor of philosophy talking about (as he might put it) "the Body/Mind dichotomy" and the drug squad detective saying "We're bringing in the body" somewhere find a meeting place. Their concerns overlap. Nothing is so puzzling as a death. The detective wants to solve the crime, if it's a crime. The philosopher wants to penetrate the mystery of life and death. He may tell you he doesn't, but he does. They both speak for us. There is the body, wedged face upward between the rock and the manuka log, the fresh cold clear stream water flowing over and around it. The detective wants to know how this happened and who's responsible. The professor is asking how did this thing which was so-and-so become *not* so-and-so. How did he become this silent biodegradable soon-to-be-nothing? How (because modern philosophers focus on language) did *he* become *it*.

We want to know these things too. We are the detective and we are the philosopher. Like them we're always asking ourselves the big questions. And like them we get mostly very small and unsatisfactory answers.

I begin in Auckland in October – a recent October. Harry Butler is having lunch with Louise Lamont. Harry Butler is the professor of philosophy. Louise Lamont is one of the four women mentioned above. She's a postgraduate research student. She's also what in earlier times you would have called Harry's mistress. These days if you were trying to avoid that word but still wanted to describe their relationship with a sort of old-world decorum, you might say they went to bed together, but that won't do either. They've very seldom been together in a bed. Mostly (as Louise would put it) they fuck on the floor.

There's a problem in telling a story. Things have to come one at a time, as through a narrow gate. But in reality nothing is single. A whole set of facts and circumstances march abreast. You have to let me build up those facts and circumstances in my own way. Have patience, give me time, and I promise I will give you a story.

I've sometimes thought about how you would begin if you were making a movie. There's a view you get looking up the slope across the park to the university where Harry teaches. At about 9.30 in the morning (it must vary with the seasons) the sun cuts through the fountain at the park centre and makes the jets of water look like some kind of rippling metal. The movie could start there – that curious watermetal effect continuously rippling while the title and credits ran down one side of the screen. Then I might cheat a bit. The camera could swing slowly around and by the time it had done a circuit of the park, taking in the bandstand, the Moreton Bay figs, the tall palms, the kowhais in bloom (it's October remember) and the spring flowers around the statue of Queen Victoria, the hour would have advanced to twelve thirty or one. Now the camera is pointing down the slope through the trees to that verandah lunch place in the Art Gallery building. Harry Butler and Louise Lamont are having lunch under a big red umbrella. For the purpose of the movie I might put a bottle of wine between them, and maybe a waiter with a white cloth over one arm. In fact you can't get wine there, and you serve yourself.

As the camera zooms in on them through the trees you see that Louise is a good-looking, well-dressed, I suppose slightly conventional young woman. What I mean by that is not exactly a rejection of feminism (there will be times, Louise knows, when every woman needs it); but if you notice the Paris label on the wide-sleeved padded jacket, or the biscuity Italian shoes, or the eye-liner and nail polish, or the hair style – or if you notice none of these things separately but gather in a fast impression of them – you can see that although she may well be a modern young woman who's not going to let a professor of philosophy, married with two children, call her his "mistress", she probably won't argue about being his "lover", and she will do all, or anyway most, of the things an old-fashioned mistress would have done. Whether she knows it or not, she wants the same things and she will suffer the same victories and defeats. This I suppose is a roundabout way of saying that – for all her protestations of "freedom" – Louise is in love with Harry Butler.

So already there are problems. But I start with this lunch because it's a moment of calm when all the good things between them are flourishing. Being professor and

6

research student may be the cover for their lunch together, but you wouldn't be deceived by it. Her fingers creep over his on the table. Under the table her foot (that elegant Italian shoe, which you may guess he bought) is rubbing the inside of his calf. They're exchanging very brief remarks which trigger laughter. That means a shared language, a private store of reference. The voices keep dropping to an undertone, and at the same time they look around to see they're not being overheard. And she's finding it difficult to keep her hands off him. At least once, in a "to hell with it" moment, she reaches across the table and spreads her fingers over his shirt front.

You know the signs, I'm sure. How you respond to them is up to you. You may be bored, irritated, disapproving, nostalgic, sympathetic, pleased, concerned. Any of these and half a dozen others is perfectly appropriate. What there can be no doubt about is what you're seeing: a man in his forties and a woman not much more than half his age, trying and failing to conceal what they're doing to one another's chemistry.

The occasion is Harry Butler's birthday. Maybe not the very day, but close to it. So Louise has been dealing with the perennial problem of the secret lover of a married man. How does she find a present special enough to make him feel loved (as he is), and which he can either hide or pretend to have bought for himself? Think not only of the practical problem, but of its moral ramifications!

Louise has solved it in what is probably the classic manner. Every old-fashioned mistress with flair would have done the same. She has bought something simple, inexpensive and small, which took her imagination. Something she would like to keep, or be given. It's a glass prism which he can put on his desk – maybe use for a paperweight. To go with it she has made a card by pasting a large and beautiful French postage stamp on a piece of stiff yellow paper, and on the opposite fold she has copied in black ink an inscription in German to the effect that he is locked in her heart for ever and the key has been thrown away. He's pleased, of course, and he finds just the right things to say. This is probably the "to hell with it" moment, when her hand spreads over his shirt front, the palm moving slowly while she stares into his eyes.

Is there any need to describe Louise in detail? I think she could be any good-looking, lively, intelligent young woman. As Verlaine says in the poem about his recurring dream, "Is she brunette, blonde or red-head? – I'm not sure". Middle height – anywhere at all, in fact, between Julietta Massina and Vanessa Redgrave. Fashionably dressed, but casual, so you can see a senior research student is one of the things she might be. Would you find her in an anti-tour rally if the Springboks came again to New Zealand? Certainly. Would she do a turn at the Rape Crisis Centre? Unlikely – it doesn't seem like her scene. Would she join the Philosophy Department Women's Collective? No she wouldn't. But she does believe in her freedom. Like so many women before her, Louise believes she belongs to the first wave of the truly emancipated.

What about Harry Butler? I would probably flatter him a little in the casting. Like putting wine on the table and adding a waiter with a white cloth, it's a case of making everything visible, and it has to be clear why a woman twenty years younger finds him attractive. So let's say our film-Harry is still athletic, the bits of grey in his hair are pretty well concealed in the original blond, his eyes are intelligent and alert, he uses his voice confidently, he says clever things. If all that is not absolutely true, it's not too far from the truth; and (more important) it matches Harry as he appears to Louise.

That, then, is our scene. We have them sitting out on the terrace, eating lunch, drinking wine, opening the present under the red umbrellas. The glass prism catches the light. The straw-coloured Italian shoe gently rubs Harry's calf.

What about dialogue? Probably in reality it was pretty basic, of the "Darling it's beautiful" and "Darling I wish I could buy you a *real* present" kind. And then I imagine they made their way up the hill for a quick turn (or maybe a long one) on the carpeted floor of the small seminar room to which Harry didn't even allow Edith, his senior secretary, a key.

Don't, I should urge you, jump to quick conclusions about Harry Butler. Hold your fire. Remember that collection of facts and circumstances waiting, each of them, to get its turn. There was, for example, the second Mrs Butler, Claire as most people still called her, but who had recently, at least inwardly, changed her name to Sophia. Could our cameras even do a quick and unexplained dash across Auckland to number 29 Arvon Crescent, Mission Bay, where she sits cross-legged in the little room that was once intended as Harry's study (he was going to write the definitive book on the Mind/Body conundrum) and which is now a sort of Sufi shrine? There our cameras would find Claire (inwardly Sophia) lost in space, rocking slowly backwards and forwards, chanting quietly "I am not this body I am not this body I am not this body . . ."

Could that rocking movement even be somehow interlocked with the different but not unrelated rhythm on the carpeted floor of the small seminar room?

9

THREE

Windows and Cameras

The Matisse poster bought to decorate my London room shows a sash window. Through the window you can see a phoenix palm, in green and gold, with a blue sky beyond. The palm fronds shower outward and fill the frame of the window. Down the right of the picture runs a curtain with a pattern of leaves in red, green and black. Below the window there is a dish of pale brown fruit. Although the phoenix palm blocks out most of the sky, the dish of fruit casts a heavy black shadow on the table.

This poster I have hung to the right of my only window, a large one looking out over the iron railing of a balcony into enormous trees which are showering leaves down over the square. Between the poster and the window hangs a green curtain. In front of the window there is a desk, with a lamp, a glass ashtray, a black Japanese radio, and a blue typewriter. There are also papers lying about, and the blue folder, talkative and waiting to be filled.

I think it was Virginia Woolf who said her worst problem as a writer was to get a character from one room to the next. Was she to write "So-and-so got up from his chair and crossed the room to the door, pausing only to notice for the first time that the kowhai was in flower"? There you feel the words going one at a time in file. And there's a similar effect you get in movies: character gets up from chair, pauses to look out (shot of kowhai in golden flower), moves on, and at the end of however many wasted frames you have him in the next room.

But on the other hand, in reality people don't flash from point A to point B like a lizard up a wall. Whichever way you choose, the slow progress or the sudden leap, it will never seem quite satisfactory.

In my own case I want to get Harry Butler across Auckland to that eastern suburb where Sufi Sophia who was Claire when she became his second wife has finished her "I am not this body" routine and is talking at her front door to two men, one in his forties, one in his twenties, both in leather jackets and blue jeans. My notion (still for a moment playing with the idea of how it might appear as a movie) is not to plod behind Harry as he makes his way there but rather to send the camera team on ahead. By the time they've set themselves up (it's always a slow business) Harry will have given a lecture and a tutorial, written a memorandum for Appointments Committee, marked a couple of essays, made a few notes for tomorrow morning's lecture, and listened to a complaint from two of the Philosophy Department Women's Collective (like nuns in the old days they always come in pairs) about sexist bias in the examples set in a recent test in Symbolic Logic. He will have put a few more essays into his bag for marking this evening, and a new book on Wittgenstein which he knows he won't read, and set off at the usual time down Grafton Road, up the steep path through trees on the Domain slope, then down Ayr Street to Shore Road where the Porsche is parked most mornings so he will have some exercise coming and going. By the time the Porsche has climbed Kepa Road and is descending towards Mission Bay he will probably be thinking about his two boys and the sailboat he's planning to buy them for Christmas. He will also be hungry, and wondering which of her six principal vegetarian dishes Claire is preparing for them, or whether, in one of those excesses of "not being" which have sometimes invaded her lately, she will have prepared nothing at all.

But if Harry's thoughts about Claire are often despairing and occasionally bitter, they shouldn't be allowed to determine what we see. Harry at this moment is no objective witness. When Claire was his favourite young Arts graduate, and he an exciting 33-year-old lecturer recently elevated to the second Professorship in Philosophy (his elevation and the end of his first marriage occurred at more or less the same time) the word he used most often in speaking about her was style. She had style in dress, in conversation, in the way she wrote, in the way she decorated a room. Now it has become one of the disciplines of her Path to Perfection to rid herself as far as possible of thoughts about appearances. Cleanliness and a decent anonymity are what her guru recommends. In particular the body-she-is-not should not be adorned and pampered. It shouldn't be indulged. It (and IT is how he teaches her to think of it) is to be kept in good running order – no more than that – because it's the temporary residence of the spirit which he has renamed Sophia.

But the sense of style if you have it isn't easily suppressed. Saris are no escape from elegance; and for Claire Butler to choose colours that clash would require a moral strenuousness alien to Sufi thought. Even those six principal vegetarian dishes are like six themes on which she plays beautiful variations. If Harry hates them it's because of what they represent, not because he doesn't enjoy them as meals. Sometimes when Claire is away he

12

cooks steak and chips and swears the boys to secrecy.

What our camera team has found in Mission Bay is what the real estate advertisements would describe as "spacious bungalow, sheltered, elevated, with sea views". While they're waiting for Harry we can imagine them ranging about with inquisitive eyes, as such teams do. They've gone out on to the verandah at the front and looked out over the roofs of lower Mission Bay across the harbour entrance and past North Head to the island of Rangitoto. That's a bit of scenery anyone might use, and not to their taste for the present purpose. They've wandered about in the sitting room, tried the big white chairs for comfort, admired the paintings on the wall, noticed the wind-harp and the cabbalistic signs hanging in the open windows. They've taken a quick, slightly embarrassed glance around the little room with the incense and flowers and the shrine; and a more relaxed look at the bathroom, spacious, all green and white, with ferns and pot-plants inside, and outside, through the open window, tree-ferns and papyrus and a grapevine putting on new leaf.

But it's in the kitchen we have to imagine them setting up their equipment to record Harry's entry. This is the same kitchen we began with, modern, well-equipped, with that machine on the sink bench for grinding carrots to make a health-giving drink. Claire Butler is pushing carrots into it with a stick. As each carrot goes through there's a painful grinding shriek, and Claire's two boys, Jonah and Reuben, sitting on the floor with muddy knees up and school socks down, pull faces and put their hands over their ears.

The kitchen table where the family eats breakfast and sometimes lunch is at a side window. Behind the table there's a bench where the boys would normally be if they chose to sit in the kitchen, but on the bench at this moment sits one (the older one) of the two leather-jacketed men we caught a glimpse of talking to Claire at the front door. He has the curtain partly drawn over the window and he's peering through the gap towards the house next door, which is set back further from the road than the Butlers' and a little further up the slope that rises from Mission Bay. The house next door is of more recent design than the Butlers' – two floors suspended on steel girders with a flat roof, a lot of glass at the front, and a spacious balcony looking down to the sea.

Banana palms have grown up in front of it, and an enormous vine which when it was planted would have been called a chinese gooseberry but is now a kiwi fruit.

The leather-jacketed man on the bench by the window has a pair of binoculars in his hands (he doesn't appear to be using them) and an RT crackling at his elbow on the table. Now and then without taking his eyes from the gap in the curtains, he says something to his younger colleague who is standing leaning over the top of the refrigerator, sighting a camera with a long lens past Claire, bent over the grinder, towards that next-door balcony on which someone has just appeared and is looking down towards the sea. In a lull between carrots the man at the window is heard to say "That's our Greg, pal", and from the top of the refrigerator comes the answering whirr and click of the shutter.

This is the scene Harry Butler comes home to. He goes around the side of the house, stops to pick caterpillars off the grapevine, and comes in by the back door and through to the kitchen. He sees first the shoes and socks and muddy knees of Jonah and Reuben. The boys lean forward as they hear him come in. Their faces are eager, excited. The young man leaning over the refrigerator doesn't move, and Harry has to go around his legs. He's still pointing his Pentax at the house next door. The one at the window looks toward Harry, then back to the gap in the curtain, then back to Harry again. Claire is turning from the grinder, drying her hands.

"Oh there you are," she says. "We've got visitors."

Then, seeing the expression on his face, she laughs. "It's all right," she says. "It's not a hi-jack. Come into the other room and I'll explain."

FOUR

Spiro Agnew and the Fait Accompli

So now, under way and under instruction, we take off for Milan in the gathering autumn. The flight is late, and later. We apologize for the delay. We ask you (as they do over the intercom) to bear with us. I would have preferred to remain in the room in London, brightened by the Matisse poster and another by Dufy. But the voice from the blue folder has never faltered: Milan (and sometimes, affecting the language, Milano). And now that the folder contains some pages, the voice is more confident. Obedient to its petulant instruction we board flight BA 512 and wait.

This is not the best season for travelling to northern Italy. That country between the Mediterranean and the mountains is prone to autumn fogs. This, and an Italian air-controllers' go-slow, explains the delay. When the pilot ("This is your Captain speaking") comes on board he tells us the man scheduled for the flight lacked the necessary flying hours to qualify for a fog landing. Hence the further delay, and the new Captain, who has a soothing Scottish accent. The announcement is meant to assure us that British Airways doesn't allow just any person to fly its planes in hazardous conditions. What it communicates is that the conditions are hazardous.

Nice food. French wine. Why not drink if you're going to die? But I don't believe for a moment that I'm going to die. I just like the wine. I feel safe because of that voice out of the blue folder. It's so commanding, it must have some

16

knowledge of the Order of Things, some link-in to the eternal terminal. It says Milan and it says now, so here we go.

But not without uncertainties. Already it's 10 p.m. and the Captain tells us, after the seat-belt and oxygen drill, that there's fog ahead and we won't know until we reach the French–Italian border whether we're to land at Milan, Genoa or Turin.

Milan, says the blue folder, and of course the blue folder is right; but the airport is Malpensa, not Linate, so we have a long bus ride in, through foggy woods and frosty fields. My hotel is the Bernina near the station; but next day I move to the Palazzo delle Stelline – the palace of the little stars – in the Corso Magenta.

Here it is I'm to give you your first proper look at Detective Larson Snow of the Auckland police drug squad. For the moment let's stand back from him and see him in action.

So we could have him, for example, getting up from his desk and walking to the door, pausing at the window to look down four floors into a paved yard. He's not noticing the kowhais because there aren't any. The best we could do along these lines would be to have him reflect that if anyone had thought of planting kowhais down there they would be flowering now.

But I don't believe that at this moment he's thinking about flowers. His mind is occupied with two young persons (as he might describe them officially – otherwise two young shits), Greg Carey and Mandy Rivers, and the house they're renting at 27 Arvon Crescent which happens to be next door to, and conveniently visible from, number 29, owned and occupied by Professor Harry Butler and his wife Claire and their two little boys Jonah and Reuben.

17

In the next room Larson Snow's young assistant, John Sprott, comes to meet him. "Here it is. Harold Avery Butler. I've just pulled him out of the computer. He's got a conviction. Disorderly behaviour."

Larson Snow looks at it. "You see the date," he says. "Know what that means? Spiro Agnew."

Probably he enjoys the look of puzzlement on John Sprott's face. "Sounds like a disease doesn't it. Pack your camera, pal. We're off to Mission Bay."

Young Sprott is silent as they drive down through the city to the waterfront. He pulls the back off his camera and puts it together again.

"I don't suppose one disorderly counts," he says.

"It counts all right. One really respectable conviction – it can do you a lot of good in some quarters. Heard of the Vietnam war? Our Harold Avery Butler was opposed. You follow? Spiro Agnew was Richard Nixon's vice president. Came here to screw some more troops out of New Zealand. He was staying at the Intercontinental up by the university. They got itchy up there. Started chucking eggs and lying down in the road."

John Sprott nods. He looks as if he has his own opinion of people like that.

They're bowling along the Waterfront Drive past the Parnell Baths and the White Heron Motel. Sprott lights two cigarettes and gives one to his boss.

"Remember," Larson says. "No heavy stuff. Smile nicely at Mrs B and we'll present the prof with a fait accompli when he gets home." He takes the cigarette and draws on it. "Fait accompli," he says. "That's another American vice president."

"Piss off Larson," John Sprott says.

They're coming to the old pumping station now. On

18

the seaward side the huge vaults under the road that used to be holding tanks for the sewage outfall are being converted into a shark aquarium.

At Mission Bay they turn inland. The streets turn this way and that, climbing. "All very nice," Larson says, nodding at the houses. "You've got to be a prof or a pusher to live up here. You know our Harold Birdcage Butler drives a Porsche?"

They put the camera gear, the RT and binoculars into a canvas hold-all that's supposed to look like something an electrician or a carpenter might carry.

Claire Butler answers the door wearing a dark blue sari and pushing a strand of hair back from her face.

Larson explains they're police and shows his card. "Nothing to be alarmed about," he says. "We've come to ask a favour."

She invites them in. He sits opposite her in a big white armchair. While they talk John Sprott wanders about the room looking at the paintings and at the view of the house next door.

"We lost track of Greg Carey for three or four years," Larson explains. "Then we started to get reports from Australia. He was part of the Mr Asia set-up. He survived the bust but we didn't know that. We thought he was dead. Then just a fortnight ago we got reports of him in Auckland. He's leasing the house next door. Number 27. It's an expensive lease and he doesn't have a job."

Claire Butler frowns. "I'm not sure I want to hear all this."

"Best view's from the kitchen," John Sprott says coming back into the room.

"I just wanted to explain why it's important," Larson says.

19

"It's important to you," she says.

"It's important to everyone, Mrs Butler. These people create their own customers. You have children. One day they could be the victims."

"Yes," she says. "Anything's possible. But if you see it from the perspective of eternity . . ."

"Oh well – eternity." He shrugs. "That's a nice address."

Claire Butler laughs. "I don't do this detachment business very well."

After a moment he says "I have to do my job. It's like hunting. First you just watch. If you blast away with both barrels before you're sure what you've got in your sights you just scare off the game."

She says she would rather he talked to her husband about it. "I'm not supposed to be thinking about worldly things."

"Does your husband tell you what you're supposed to think about?"

She shakes her head. "No. Not at all. I'm trying to be a Sufi. I have a kind of teacher."

"So what would your teacher tell you to do about us?"

"I've been wondering. He might say 'Render unto Caesar . . .' "

Larson nods. "Good." From the kitchen comes the whirr and click of John Sprott's camera.

"What about the boys," she asks. "They'll be home from school soon."

"You just tell them not to talk about it. Kids like a secret. And they like our gear. A family's good cover for us."

"Well," she says. "I'd rather Harry decided. But if you want to you can watch until he comes home."

So Larson Snow gets his fait accompli. They set up their gear in the kitchen. Larson puts himself at the side window. There's a big lassiandra bush in front of it. He can see through it, and he knows its leaves and purple flowers are reflected in the glass, concealing him from anyone in the garden. But he closes the curtain half way across, to make sure.

The big plate glass windows in number 27 make it easy to see inside. Grey Carey is in there. His flashy sports is in the carport, and a couple of times Larson sees him pass across the rear of the balcony from one room to another. But not long enough for a picture.

The Butler boys, Jonah and Reuben, arrive home from school. There is excitement, and explanations. They're given a carrot each and they sit side by side on the floor eating them.

An Alfa Romeo comes into the drive of number 27 and stops just short of the carport. Larson is pleased.

"He's a lawyer of sorts," he tells Claire. "Where there's drugs there's Macready. It's smoke and fire."

John Sprott is working his camera hard while Larson phones through to Central the message that Macready has turned up at 27 Arvon Crescent.

A few minutes later Macready comes out again. He stands for a moment with his car door open, staring around the garden and the nearby houses.

"Hold it like that," John Sprott says, sighting across the top of the refrigerator.

A girl comes out on the balcony and watches him get into his car. She gives only the faintest wave as he drives off. She's tall, with light brown hair that looks almost blond in the sun.

"Her name's Mandy," Reuben says. "She's nice."

21

"Mandy," Larson repeats. "That's the one."

Ten minutes of nothing. The boys are getting restless. Claire is pushing carrots into the grinder. The noise rises to an ugly pitch. For a moment or two Larson is distracted by it. Then a movement up at the big house catches his eye. The ranchslider opens and a young man comes out on the balcony and stands looking down towards the sea.

"That's our Greg, pal," Larson says, and once again John Sprott works hard with his camera.

This is the moment already described. Harry Butler walks in to find his family in the kitchen, together with two men in blue jeans and black leather jackets.

Claire turns from the grinder, drying her hands. "Oh there you are," she says. "We've got visitors." And then, seeing the expression on his face, she laughs. "It's all right. It's not a hi-jack. Come into the other room and I'll explain."

FIVE

Trackback and the Padrone

I have now to track back a bit. Characters aren't just names and faces. They have histories which they bring with them like awkward luggage. How is it (and how much of it is) to be got through that narrow gate?

I said this was a story about three men. Mostly it's Harry Butler's story. But along with him go two others, Jason Cook and Phil Gardner. They were at school together. Harold Avery Butler. Jason Illingworth Cook. And Philip Lundquist Gardner. And for good measure there was that favourite English master known to the school as "Old Stew" who made them a group, a gang of three before they'd quite recognized that that was what they were, when he referred to them as the Butler, the Gardner and the Cook.

We've seen Harry Butler already. But we've also seen Jason Cook – only briefly, in our opening scene. He was the one who was about to be shot over the top of the refrigerator by John Sprott's long lens, and buried in drug squad files, when Harry Butler put himself in the way. Harry made a scene. He pretended he'd had enough of the drug squad cluttering up his kitchen. They'd been in the house ten days or a fortnight so it was plausible, and I don't suppose at that moment either Larson Snow or John Sprott guessed that Harry's tantrum had anything to do with the face out there they were trying to borrow for the

record. Instead of Jason's face they got Harry's shirt-front.
It was of grey and darker grey, in stripes (Harry had a taste
for greys that year) and of course it was out of focus.

This is a scene we will no doubt come back to. Expected
time of arrival? God knows we have no clear expectations,
only hopes, struggling first in London, now in a little café
on the Corso Magenta, Milan, to pack and unpack, to
label and marshal through the narrow gate of language,
the luggage of that past. There's a special look comes into
the eyes of the café owner, signalling it will cost me
another cup of coffee to keep my place at this table. It
reminds me I mustn't be random with my facts.

So I try to settle on the one thing that might explain
why they were a gang of three, not of two or four. I don't
find it of course. They were three boys pretty much like
any other three. There was no sentimental pact or blood
brotherhood, as in *Beau Geste* or *The Last of the Mohicans*,
though probably they read those books. If they were
brothers it was only in the way those modern women who
insist on being sisters so disapprove of. They were "the
boys". Having fun was what they did together, and it led
to a kind of instant loyalty, like a reflex. So it was Harry's
shirt-front and not Jason's face that went into drug squad
files.

Not all the fun was lawful. There was a year when Jason
took to borrowing cars. He'd learned how to hot-wire an
engine; and in those days it was easy to get under the
bonnet of a car.

And there was the summer when they set hedges on
fire. Not many hedges – two at least, and possibly three.
One was in Remuera, in front of a big house which Jason
afterwards told them belonged to his mother who (he said)
drank sherry all day and owned shares in South African

24

diamond mines. But since Jason liked to embroider the truth, and sometimes even to invent it, neither Harry nor Phil knew whether to believe him.

Jason was the best debater in the school. Harry used to think it was because he didn't believe in anything, and he had style. Waiting to go into an exam Jason could usually be heard asking them for "something to say". If he had something to say he could be relied on to say it well.

Phil was more pedestrian. He was the note-taker, the one who read the text-book and didn't miss classes. It was Phil who supplied Jason with a few scraps of fact which Jason could blow up into something insubstantial but elegant, like a soufflé.

Harry was somewhere between the two. He didn't work as hard as Phil, but he had a good memory, and he was clear and logical. Sometimes his logic was a strength; other times he seemed to get trapped inside it.

They were successful at school and they drifted on, for lack of any other direction, towards university. Jason lasted there only a couple of terms. He was seen irregularly in green corduroy and brown suede shoes. He wrote an essay for his English tutor about the nature of fiction. It was called "O Henry James Joyce Cary", and his tutor told him if he would only take himself and his subject seriously he might have a future as an academic. By now Jason was acting in a play. On the basis of that performance he was advised to get himself to RADA in London as soon as possible because there might be a future for him in the theatre. Armed with these two pieces of encouragement, and leaving a couple of elegant little poems to be published in a student literary magazine, Jason took a job with a trainer of trotting horses at Takanini. He referred to his only publication, those two poems, as "posthumous"

Jason Cook the aesthete was going underground. Occasional letters and Christmas cards went back and forth, but I think it's unlikely Harry Butler or Phil Gardner saw him again for five or six years.

In that time they both graduated, Harry in Philosophy, Phil in English. Harry's scholarship took him to Oxford. Phil worked for a time on an Auckland newspaper, then went to London. They were soon meeting again, sometimes in London, sometimes in Oxford. They weren't entirely at ease with one another. It was because they were both trying to be something they were not. Harry was becoming the Oxford man. He'd won a blue, and been elected to a club, and all the rest of it. Phil was adopting the shabby corduroy and tweed look of the literary journalist of those days. He lived in digs in north London, drank in a pub near the BBC, and thought he'd been nodded to once or twice by Louis MacNeice. They were both working on their vowels – a sort of grinding down and buffing up was going on somewhere in the back of the mouth, like gemstones in a West Coast river. In one another's company they felt embarrassed and gave up the effort. Like most New World expatriates they were full of contradictions, mixing contempt for the country of their birth with sentimental reminiscence and nostalgia.

I have to keep hold of these two. The café owner has joined me at the table with a small black poisonous coffee into which he's poured some grappa. He wants to know what is the point of all this. I tell him it's necessary background. He asks when we will get to the body (I made the mistake of mentioning there's to be a body). I tell him not yet – not for a long time. He's not interested in books as such – he doesn't have time for reading, he tells me. But a movie, that's different. He watches late night movies on

26

television in the café when the customers are thinning out. "Give me a scene," he says, holding his palms open across the table. "Background. Foreground. I don't care. But a scene please Maestro."

So I riffle through my notes and come up with the following. The place is the village of Sallanches in the French Alps. Harry and Phil are walking up the steep winding road above the village with Natalie, the young French woman who was to be Harry's first wife. I don't think I need to describe her. She was quite beautiful, so you can cast her in your own image of the beautiful Frenchwoman. But Catherine Deneuve rather than Brigitte Bardot – and in her early twenties. The weather is fine and wonderfully clear, the road is very steep, there's the sound of cow bells coming up from the pastures below the road, the snow on the mountain peaks looms over. As they walk they're eating apples and plums picked from trees along the roadside. They're looking for a mountain café where they can sit out and enjoy the scene. But as they pant on up the road Harry is trying to explain to Natalie what Descartes said about the Mind/Body puzzle. Her English is limited, his French is worse. In English she can't grasp the complexities of the argument. And after all, Descartes was French. Can't he tell her (this is her complaint) what Descartes *really* said? So he tries, but he gets his tenses wrong, he mixes genders, he loses the thread. They're both frustrated, then angry, and finally silent. The coffee when they get to it has a bitter flavour, and there's mist coming down over the peaks.

The padrone holds his hand out flat, palm down, and tilts it this way and that. He likes the scenery but not the dialogue. And he wants to know – this French Natalie who married the Mind/Body Harry – was she Catholic?

27

Is he taking me away from my subject or towards it? I try to explain that Natalie was an only child – that seems more important than her Catholicism. In fact I give him another scene. It's the home of Natalie's parents, on the outskirts of Châlon – an old stone house with a farmhouse clock that strikes the hour not once but twice. The reason for the twice chiming is that you never start counting soon enough so the clock gives you a second chance. Harry dislikes it. It keeps him awake at night. He dislikes everything about these visits (he and Natalie are now married) except drinking the wine of the countryside. He dislikes his mother-in-law, whom he refers to as Mother Nourriture or Madame Alimentation because of the large meals she insists they eat to improve their fertility. She suspects, and she's right, that her daughter and this *philosophe* husband (who speaks French like a Spanish cow) are obstructing the natural processes. Harry wants to know why a woman who produced only one child should be so insistent about her daughter's fertility. His French may be that of a Spanish cow but it's understood, and it's the wrong question at the wrong moment. Now the mother-in-law is in tears. Now the daughter is remonstrating. Now the father is taking Harry's part. Now the two women have turned on the father. Now the clock is chiming, not once but twice. "Oh shit," Harry is saying, and probably "*Merde*" for good measure. "Let's for Christ's sake go and live in New Zealand."

I don't pretend that this explains their decision, but sometimes a single scene has to stand for many. They'd been over and through and around the question. Harry liked to visit France but he liked to leave it too. He didn't want to live in Paris, and Natalie didn't want to live in London. She'd listened in on his and Phil's nostalgia sessions; and she said she'd always been interested in "ze sous seas". Phil thought she'd inherited that French romanticism which took Gaugin off to the Pacific. He said nothing to Harry (Phil was discreet), but he wrote to Jason that someone ought to make her look at those despairing empty brown faces Gaugin painted when he got there, and ask her why she thought in one of those pictures he stuck Edgar Allan Poe's raven on the window sill and the word *Nevermore*.

The padrone interrupts at this point. Why was the raven on the window sill? Who is this Edgar Allenpoe?

I don't try to explain. I just rush him on to another scene or two. Harry and Natalie are sailing into Auckland harbour. The camera sweeps around and there it is – still, really, a port in "ze sous seas". All those wooden bungalows with red iron roofs. And the beaches, the yachts, the islands of the Gulf, the green volcanic hills, the gardens, the flowers, the tall sky, the searching light, the marvellous air. O Corso Magenta – across the street in the church of Santa Maria delle Grazie you are trying to restore to its former glory Leonardo's *Last Supper*. Any day an Auckland sky can repaint itself twice over, and with the hand of a master.

The padrone's no intellectual but he protests, and he's right. What about the big black raven and Edgar Allenbow's despair? That too, that too, I'm forced to admit. I'm a long way from home, signor. Excuse a moment of nostalgia. It will serve anyway to illustrate what Natalie might have heard from Harry and Phil.

And it isn't as if their emigration was a disaster at once. Natalie could be shown, for example, throwing her arms about dancing wildly in the west coast surf, or leaning into the wind that races over the dunes and through the marram grass, shouting Francophone superlatives at the landscape. She could be shown in tramping boots and very short shorts climbing a track through kauris and rimus, or down through one of those patches where nikau and karaka combine overhead to intensify the greenness of the bush light. And there's at least one snap-shot of her, obviously happy, at Phil's wedding in Auckland (Phil wasn't long in following them home) where she met the mysterious and now very elegant Jason for the first time.

But it wasn't going to work and it didn't. To her it seemed the houses of Auckland were always open but the people remained shut. The accent was unfamiliar and her problems with the language got worse. Summer passed and it seemed always to be raining. Harry worked long hours. He grew anxious and irritable. She missed her loving parents and the stone house and the twice-chiming clock. It was said of her, as it's said of most migrants, that she was difficult, complained too much, wasn't grateful. (The descendants of settlers have buried the trauma of transplantation. They don't want it dug up in every generation.) And in addition Natalie was French. At first that was an advantage. It was chic. But as people got used to it they grew impatient of her Gallic inflexibility.

And I have to admit, when the padrone presses me on this point, that Claire was already in the wings before Natalie had left the stage. Harry met her at a student party, things were bad at home, and he was bowled over by the way she talked, the way she dressed, and (before long) by the letters she wrote him in very black ink decorated around the edges with little sketches. She'd already finished her BA in which she'd taken only one unit in Philosophy because (she told him) she hadn't approved of his lectures on Body/Mind. He found this frankness

30

charming, he enjoyed the argument that followed, and he didn't tell her he thought her mystical notions had more to do with the fashion for flower-power than with logic or insight. It didn't occur to him then, or for a very long time afterwards, that students don't always grow out of the fashions of their youth. Sometimes they grow into them.

As Harry's friendship with Claire developed into an affair, all reasonable judgements became irrelevant. He could listen to her talk about the "actionless act", or the mystical properties of the number 8, or the penumbra of yellow she caught sight of sometimes when he bent over her, as if it was some kind of music, or poetry. And in any case, to talk of their friendship growing into an affair is like saying the wind is getting stronger when it has just knocked down the house. There are, obviously, some scenes I could put before the padrone at this point but he seems a conventional northern Italian and I don't think he would want anything too explicit on his screen. I simply adopt what I think he might see as a kind of Roman weariness, and tell him love was a word you could use safely when talking about Harry and Natalie. With Harry and Claire, in those heady early days of their first knowing one another, it had to be something stronger. Passion, for example. Or insanity.

SIX

Neutral Eyes

The padrone in the Café Corso Magenta has got used to me. He makes me welcome. I no longer feel I need to drink coffee at the rate of Balzac to earn my place at his table. It's my place of work, and that's accepted. I like my room in the Palazzo delle Stelline; but I prefer not to live and work in the same room.

I get to the café in the morning when the padrone still has the chairs up and is sweeping out, or washing the last of the dishes from the night before. He has my table in the corner near the window ready. When he has finished cleaning he makes me my first cup of coffee. I'm left alone then for about an hour and a half. About 11.30 the Consul's wife comes in. I have a cup of coffee with her and we talk about my work. Her Italian is good so she's able to act as interpreter and answer some of the things the padrone wants to know about the story which I haven't been able to explain.

Why Milan? I still don't know the answer to that, but for the moment the blue folder is uncomplaining, I have the right conditions in which to work, I have the padrone and the Consul's wife – not friends, who might interfere or distract me, but company to humanize my day. Perfect working conditions you might say, and insofar as that's true I know it won't last. I try to make the most of it.

My attitude to the Consul's wife is difficult to describe.

She's tall, blond, good-looking, shapely. She's what I think of as bourgeois. By that I mean not only that she shows all the signs of affluence you would expect of a Consul's wife; she also gives the impression of never having known anything else.

Her name is Uta Haverstrom, and her husband is Consul of one of the Scandinavian countries. I'm not sure which, and just at the moment I feel reluctant to ask because that would mean admitting I don't know. That reveals something of my attitude to her. Though she's a lot younger than I am, I feel nervous of her. When she asks questions about my work I feel an edge in my voice that's like the tone in which a schoolboy answers a teacher. She's some kind of monitor. Yet I'm glad of her questions. There's something immediate and close about the freedom she feels to ask them; and answering helps to clear my mind.

So she wants to know, for example, whether Larson Snow is to be seen as the unsubtle and insensitive cop, and that question forces me to think about him. I decide he's neither unsubtle nor insensitive, but that he has put on a show of being both, so long and so successfully it comes almost to the same thing.

Larson had started off in the drug squad with the idea that as well as being a hunter of evil men, he was going to be a protector of their clients. Like everyone else, he knew stories of nice kids who OD'd, talented kids who dropped out, innocent kids who became victims. He wasn't simple-minded about the job; but part of its appeal when he was shifted from regular duties was the thought that it was a kind of life-saving operation.

But the sense of being a life-saver didn't last. The victims refused to act like victims. They didn't seem to hate

33

the pushers who were living off them. They hated the drug squad who made it hard for them to get on with a quiet life of self-destruction. When they didn't have their drugs they scratched their arms and twisted inside their clothes, their noses ran and their eyes went glassy and desperate – and sometimes murderous. After a fix they turned into little saints again, drifting about in a haze of peace and love. If they had ambitions it was usually to become a Greg Carey or (the big egos) an Alexander Sinclair, but they always made a mess of it. They got in on the fringes, doing the dangerous work, carrying the stuff back from Thailand and through customs. They were caught, or they talked, sometimes they vanished, occasionally one turned up handless under an Australian sand dune or at the bottom of a river. They didn't like Larson Snow because of what he was; and he didn't like them for all the good reasons people have for not liking addicts of every kind – because they're dishonest, compulsive, unscrupulous, embarrassing, destructive, and worst of all boring. There was nothing of Mother Teresa or James K. Baxter about Larson Snow. For the Teresa touch you needed a special appetite for the afflicted; and if you had it, Larson knew, you would fail in your role as a hunter.

The hunter in him lasted longer. Being patient, being very still, not moving too soon. And then the excitement of the breakthrough or the bust. All the time you had to keep in mind that it wasn't enough to know what was going on. That was easy. The hard part was being able to prove it in a court.

But watching people for long hours, tailing them, getting to know their habits, made them familiar. You started to respond to them in a human way. Some you liked, others you disliked, and the liking or not liking didn't have much to do with how guilty they were. Sometimes the really bad ones had strengths you admired; often you felt contempt for the weaknesses of the victims. Larson Snow had once spent hours interviewing Alexander Sinclair before he made his break to Australia. Larson found him charming, intelligent, someone who looked you straight in the eye and didn't cringe or threaten. He could have been a successful businessman. Yet in the years after his escape Sinclair was said to have ordered a dozen killings, and to have carried out some of them himself.

Boredom was the enemy, and as boredom increased Larson looked forward to the moments of excitement. He liked the early morning break-ins, when the squad surrounded a house or a flat and at a signal broke down doors and were inside in twenty seconds. That was to stop heroin being flushed down a lavatory and papers being burned. But it set the adrenalin racing. It made up for the hours of doing nothing.

The trouble was you got more and more like the people you were hunting. They too led boring lives, with sudden flurries of action and danger. They too were always on the watch. It was a seedy, avid world, and it grew over you like a fine mould. That was why Larson quite liked the strange, slow-spoken Claire Butler in the dark blue sari. He was used to people whose hate showed when his identity as a drug squad detective was revealed. And he was used to good citizens, eager to be seen as good citizens, who told him how important his work was. It was nice to meet someone who sat tranquil and looked at him with neutral eyes.

SEVEN

Mandy at the Mirror

We have now to bring Larson Snow and Harry Butler together in the same room. The drug squad detective and the professor of philosophy. That's not how each thought of himself, but it's how each would think of the other.

So we go back to the professor of philosophy in his Porsche that evening descending from Kepa Road towards Mission Bay. What was on his mind? There was, as reported already, the sailboat he was going to buy Jonah and Reuben for the coming summer. There was the question, with its edge of resentment, about which of her vegetarian dishes Claire might be cooking. There must also have been thoughts about his lunch with Louise, and the glass prism, and what happened afterwards (if it happened) on the carpeted floor of the small seminar room to which he alone possessed a key. He was also thinking about the review he'd read that day in the *TLS* of a new book on the philosophy of mind, which had made some point about a chimpanzee climbing a tree because it believed there were bananas up there. As he stopped to pick caterpillars off the grapevine he wasn't thinking exactly about the review nor about the book reviewed. He was thinking he was sure chimpanzees and bananas came from different continents, and wondering which of his reference books he could look at that would tell him. Then he went indoors and found the boys on the floor with their muddy knees up, and Claire at the carrot grinder, and the kitchen seeming at a glance to be crowded with leather jackets and blue jeans.

Claire said "Oh there you are," told him it wasn't a hijack, and began to explain what was happening. For a minute or two Larson Snow and John Sprott were occupied getting shots of Greg Carey who had just come out on the balcony next door. Then Larson followed Harry and Claire into the next room. He introduced himself. He apologized for the intrusion. He explained what was going on and how essential it was to current drug squad investigations that the couple next door should be watched. He asked permission to stay for a while – he didn't say for how long, because he knew that once you were in a house you only had to behave unobtrusively and help with the dishes and the days tended to drift by unnoticed.

Harry didn't like housing the drug squad so why did he say they could stay? One of his best students had become a heroin addict. And he knew, not well, but well enough to feel pity for him, the father of a girl who'd become one of those handless corpses in Australia. Those were two good reasons, and they were the two he mentioned to Claire. But there was something else. It wasn't a reason, but it has to be part of any explanation. Living with the young man next door there was the young woman, Mandy. Reuben had picked up her name, and Larson knew it already. So did Harry, but he hadn't ever said so, and he didn't say so now. He knew the name and he knew the girl; and he'd met her in circumstances which now – in the light of the drug squad's interest – seemed full of sinister overtones.

Am I making myself less than clear? It always happens

37

when one becomes explanatory. I must trust the Story, and get on with it.

So we have what might be called a normal domestic household in the eastern suburbs of Auckland, the kitchen occupied all day and part of the night by two, sometimes three, occasionally just one, of the police drug squad. We have to see the household going about its normal routines, getting up, breakfasting, seeing the boys off to school, and so on through the day, over and around the men in leather jackets determinedly watching, taking notes and photographs, sending out messages by phone or on the RT. In the evening the dishes have to be done early, or in the dark, because a light in the kitchen would reveal the watcher who in daylight is protected by the reflection of lassiandra leaves and purple flowers on the window pane.

The routine is normal except that now everyone is watching, even Claire, who in her wish to become Sufi Sophia tries, but fails, to maintain the right kind of indifference to what's going on.

It's spring and the Auckland weather is erratic. It's mild; but conflicting orders are coming down from on high. It seems there's a certain generous issue of sunshine to be used up, and a correspondingly large one of rain. Similarly with stillness and wind. And growth. You can watch the grass coming up. It has that hectic colour which makes New Zealand movies look artificial, as if faked by some trick in the laboratory. The garden is no sooner holding itself still, smiling nicely and waiting for John Sprott's shutter to whirr and click, than a huge gust dashes across wrecking its pose, or a brilliant shower is thrown down like spears without altering at all the intensity of the light. So Greg Carey's visitors as they appear on the file are alternately rain-soaked and sun-bathed, and sometimes both at once. They come and go. Some few are known to the squad, including the lawyer Macready already observed. In one of John Sprott's photographs Macready is glancing up into a shaft of liquid light that might be coming direct to him from the big Pusher in the skies.

Jonah and Reuben are sworn to silence about all this, but they watch. Everyone in the house watches. At first Greg Carey and Mandy Rivers appear to be sinister. Then as the days go by they begin to look human and ordinary. Greg, who has a slick, well-groomed appearance, seems a weak, petulant character, always complaining. Mandy has a helpless look, as if she doesn't know whether to go or stay. She's bored and restless. There's a mirror she goes to often in the front bedroom of the house. She stares at herself. She adopts poses, putting her head to one side then the other, changing her clothes, dancing, uncovering her breasts, pouting, smiling. She goes back on to the balcony to stare down towards the sea, or through to the living room to put a record on the machine or to watch television; but after a while she goes back to the mirror. It's as if she's trying to see herself. It pleases Larson, this routine, because he says as long as she goes on doing it you can be sure they don't know they're being watched.

Harry has watched Mandy at the mirror since she and Greg first moved into the house next door. Now everyone is watching her. John Sprott amuses himself trying to get shots of her with the long lens. Jonah and Reuben giggle and nudge one another. Larson looks at her, then turns away bored and watches the grass growing. Claire sees it and feels as if she would like to protect Mandy from all these prying male eyes.

EIGHT

Mandy at the Clothes Line, Claire among Flowers

There is now the passage of several days. Let's say (to fill the gap) I have left the café and gone back along the Corso Magenta to my room in the Palazzo delle Stelline. It's a modern room, the interior of the Palace of the Little Stars, which was once an orphanage, having been entirely redesigned. I switch on my travelling radio and stand out on the balcony looking over red tiled roofs towards the yellow-orange tower of Santa Maria delle Grazie. From the radio comes one of the most beautiful passages – a trio for female voices – from Strauss's *Der Rosenkavalier*. When it's over I switch off, thinking that art is the register of a harmonious soul. I wonder whether it would mean the same to say that art is the register of a harmonious mind, and I think it very nearly would, except that the word soul seems more comprehensive, better suited to the feelings aroused in me by the music.

At the same time I have in mind images of two blind men I've seen, one in London, the other in Auckland. The one in Auckland is an athlete who runs attached by a string, wrist to wrist, to a runner who's sighted. The one in London is an American who is led about briskly on the arm of his wife. Both are good-looking men, except that they have no eyes. Both have constantly upturned faces. They are intent, listening, one sense doing duty for two.

And connected with all this is an article I read

somewhere that said quadraplegics are unable to feel powerful surges of emotion because they have no bodily sensations in which these can be registered. Such fears and ecstasies as they are able to experience remain in the head.

I don't pretend I can make sense of all these separate thoughts and images, but I know they're connected, and that they bear at least some resemblance to the thought-clusters, or in his case they might have been brain-storms, that were occurring in the head of Harry Butler during those days of the drug squad's occupation. At home, as well as the presence of Larson Snow, there was Harry's continuing estrangement from Claire in her role as Sufi Sophia. At the university there was the threatening dilemma of his affair with Louise Lamont; and there were problems connected with plans for a new Arts Faculty building in which his Department was to be housed. It was not a time when he would have been expecting to do any useful thinking as a philosopher. But in fact his thoughts were running continually on their old obsession with the Body/Mind conundrum. Maybe it was only an escape from the problems he felt beset by. Whatever the reason, there was a speeding up, and at the same time a curious blurring, of his mental processes. He felt less clarity in his thinking, but also more confidence. I don't say he could have sorted out for me and made clear the connexions between my response to the music, and my images of the blind men, and my recollection of the article about quadraplegia; but I'm sure he would have recognized the track my thoughts were taking, and he would have been able to put it into a broader philosophical picture.

But if all that seems too abstract it might be possible to convey Harry's mental state more directly by another scene. Let's approach it first from the outside, not at once attempting to report on Harry's thoughts and feelings until his behaviour seems to reveal them. At least a week has gone by since the drug squad moved in. Harry's irritation is probably beginning to show. If it is, Larson Snow is doing his best to ignore it. Breakfast is over. Jonah and Reuben have left for school. Greg Carey has driven out in his sports, and after a call to Central, Larson has sent John Sprott to follow him at a discreet distance. Claire has retired to the little room that was once Harry's study and is now her shrine. Harry comes into the kitchen dressed and ready to leave. His face has that after-shave brightness, but the expression in his eyes doesn't match it. He goes to the window and looks out. Next door Mandy is hanging out the washing under the big open carport. Larson is near the side window but he's not watching her. He's talking into the RT and listening, monitoring John Sprott's tail on Greg Carey.

Harry goes out by the back door, stops to check the grapevine, puts his bag down. He drifts over towards the next-door carport and stands on his side of the fence, not six feet from where Mandy is pegging out her underwear. In this place he's hidden from the kitchen windows by a tall thick papyrus. Harry lifts the lid of his compost bin and pokes around inside it. Without looking up he says, "How are you Mandy?"

She doesn't show any sign of having heard, but the pegging out speeds up.

"You're living dangerously," he says, still keeping his voice low.

She glances, not at him, but towards the house. Then she says, under her breath but unmistakably, "Fuck off Harry."

He puts the lid back on the compost bin. She has

finished pegging out. She's picking up the basket. "Mandy," he says. "Listen. You should clear out of here. Your friend's being watched."

And he turns and walks back towards the house.

Now he's in a state of agitation and uncertainty. He takes his bag up to the garage, raises the door, throws the bag into the car, looks at his watch (thinking of the Buildings Committee meeting he's to attend that morning), gets into the car, gets out again.

Soon he's back in the house, this time by the front door. In the little room where the definitive Mind-Body book was to have been written Claire in the dark blue sari of Sophia sits cross-legged among flowers chanting "I am not this body I am not this body I am not this body . . ."

In front of her, at the centre of the shrine, there is a clay figurine of a whirling dervish.

He shuts the door and leans against it, looking as if he wants to say something, but she doesn't stop. The chanting and the rocking continue. It strikes Harry as a strangely physical assertion of the non-corporeal.

Now Harry is moving towards her. He lowers himself to the floor and takes up a position alongside her, also cross-legged, fixing his eyes on the figure of the whirling dervish at the centre of the shrine. He too begins to rock and chant, but his mantra goes "I am this body I am this body I am this body . . ."

Possibly he begins with the intention of breaking in on her, spoiling her concentration. If so, she doesn't respond. But as he gets into the rhythm of his chant he feels soothed by it; and at the same time his mind is sitting over and above the experience, watching and commenting. So Harry is thinking that her mantra is true, but so is his; and if both are true both must be false, because they contradict one another. How can both be true and both false? Somehow language itself is failing them. But as it fails them logically it also serves its purpose, gathering up in its repetitions their sense of themselves, like thread on to a spool.

But at the same time something else is happening. Sitting side by side with the resolute Claire in the blue sari, his upper arm just brushing her shoulder as they rock forward and back, he's aware of a sort of electricity passing between them. Let's be honest, in fact, free for a moment of what you can do with a camera, and what you can tell the padrone and the Consul's wife, and say that this "electricity" is giving him an erection.

But that's not all. There is also at this moment the memory of a dream that woke him in the night. In the dream he was walking along a very narrow road past a very large, very tense and threatening dog. He didn't know whether the dog would let him pass, and he edged by slowly and apprehensively. Then, just as he was almost past, the dog hurled itself at him, as only a real dog can, all snarl and teeth and muscle. He got such a fright he jumped awake, his heart racing, his skin damp with sweat.

What he asks himself now is this: if he, Harry Butler, didn't know until it happened whether or not the dog would bite him, who did know? Who gave the dream dog autonomy to act? If his mind was author of the fiction of the dream, why did his mind not know how it was going to end? Isn't it wrong, then, to speak of one mind? On the evidence of this experience there must be at least two, one playing the dream trick on the other. And if there are two, why should there not be more?

All of this "thinking" happens, as such thoughts do, in an instant, and simultaneous with the mantras and (not least by now) the erection. And over them all a kind of excitement, a sense of headlong rush, because all parts of the experience go together, like mirrors reflecting one another.

What of Claire at this moment? That's harder. One of the great subjects of dispute between her and Harry is her guru and the advice he gives her. His name is Duag Mac-Pherson but he's known to his followers as Abd-bin-Abdal. Harry calls him the carpet seller. He has travelled in India and beyond, hob-nobbing with holy men, and now he teaches a mixture of Gurdjieff and Sufism. He teaches that most of us sleep through our earthly existence. We waste our souls in the Great Sleep of the Body. He is teaching Claire how to become truly Sophia. To achieve this she must become Awake and Aware (there are a lot of As in his teaching, as in his name). She must learn detachment from her body. She must learn to insist upon its inferior status, otherwise it will reimpose its sleep upon her soul.

At this moment, then, we can say that whereas so much is going on in Harry's mind, in hers there's nothing – or at least there's a serious attempt to achieve nothingness. She's trying to rid herself not only of her body but of rational thought which is another kind of sleep. She's trying to be her soul.

So we have our scene, in which so much and so little is happening. How long it goes on isn't clear. To Harry it seems a long time, but a time without anxiety, a sort of drifting. He feels disembodied, except that his sense of himself is drawing more and more into that centre of the stiffened phallus. He floats, weightless. His hand goes across to Claire and he pushes this way and that through the cloth of her sari. Claire doesn't resist. But neither does

45

Sophia. In fact (and probably it's the first time in many weeks) her body welcomes him. They roll over and make love on the Persian carpet among the spring flowers, and when it's over she looks up at him with an expression of languor and mild surprise. She says "I am not this body" – and she laughs.

Harry missed the meeting of the Buildings Committee that morning. It was an important meeting. Last submissions were to be made to it about the new Arts Faculty building and it was said later that Harry's Department got less than its fair share of space because he'd missed that chance to press their case. About 11 a.m. he rang his secretary, Edith, and told her he was late because he'd been unwell; but when Louise Lamont put her head around his door just before midday she remarked that he looked unusually chirpy. He told her he'd slept well (was he thinking of the Sleep of the Body?) and that he wouldn't be free to have lunch with her.

NINE

At the Consulate

Last night at Uta's invitation I dined at the Consulate. She'd given me the address, and a time, and I took a taxi from the square in front of the Castello Sforzesco.

A wrought iron gate opened by a security guard led into a courtyard surrounded by porticos and cloisters. The apartment occupied by Uta and the Consul was on the first floor.

Uta introduced me to her husband. His name is Erik Haverstrom. He's tall, in his early forties, good-looking, with dark hair greying at the edges. He's also charming, formal, rather distant in manner, well-educated and intelligent. Already he'd heard from Uta about my Professor Harry Butler. Unlike the padrone he didn't press me to say when the body would put in an appearance. What interested him was Harry Butler as a philosopher. He said from what Uta had told him it was clear that Harry was not a Dualist and that Claire was. So their marital problems were really philosophical. But he hadn't been able to work out whether Harry was a Behaviourist, a Central State Materialist, or an Epiphenomenalist.

I was embarrassed not to be able to answer these questions; and I think the Consul probably considered if I was going to put Harry Butler's story on record these were things I ought to know. Uta defended me. Wasn't it likely, she argued, that a really original philosopher wouldn't be classifiable under any such heading? Didn't originality mean that you were different from everyone who went before?

The Consul asked me whether I thought this Harry Butler was, after all, so very original in his thinking. All I could say was that there were times when he thought he was. But I had to admit as well that during this phase of his career some of Harry's colleagues believed he was becoming woolly and emotional and losing the fine clear edge that had characterized his thinking at the time when he was appointed professor.

"I think they were jealous," Uta said firmly.

Erik Haverstrom looked judicious and said nothing.

But if Uta was prepared to defend Harry's originality as a thinker, she didn't agree that the problem between him and Claire was philosophical.

"Not", she said, "as long as he has that Louise – the one he does things to on the floor."

Erik Haverstrom smiled and said nothing.

"Well why are you smiling," Uta asked. "Let us share the joke please."

The Consul shrugged. "It's just that I thought you told me his wife was the one he did something to – as you call it – on the floor."

There was such an occurrence on the floor of the shrine room – Uta conceded that. But that seemed, she said, to have been an isolated event. And anyway she wasn't quite sure my account of it would have been entirely accurate. After all, I was a man. Would Claire Butler have described it in that way? In fact it had occurred to Uta that Claire, sitting at her shrine trying to keep her mind on higher things, might not have wanted to be drawn back like that into the mechanics of her own body. Wasn't Harry forcing himself on her? Mightn't it even have been in its own quiet way a kind of rape?

I assured her it wasn't but I doubt that she was convinced.

Erik wanted me to give further examples of Harry's thinking. I said I would try, but I couldn't fit them into those categories he'd mentioned – Epiphenomenalism and all the rest of it. All I could do was tell it as it had happened.

So I described to them another morning, a little later, while the drug squad were still in occupation. Or it might have been after Harry had put his shirt in front of John Sprott's camera to stop them getting a picture of Jason, and then told them it was time they left his house.

Anyway it was morning, Harry was on his way to the university, he'd parked the Porsche down in Ayr Street and now he was walking through the Domain. Behind there was the drug squad, either present or recently evicted, and Greg Carey next door with Mandy Rivers. Also Claire, who seemed in the past few days to have suffered some remorse (and maybe a consultation with Duag Mac-Pherson) over her lapse back into the Body. Ahead was Louise Lamont, who was growing daily into that old-fashioned stereotype of the Discontented Mistress. There was also the Buildings Committee, the Dean of Arts, and the Philosophy Department Women's Collective.

In between there was the head of Harry Butler, containing them all and stuck on his body which was walking through the Auckland Domain in spring.

What's important here – because it was important to Harry – is to recognize how many different things were going on, how many thoughts and feelings and perceptions and recognitions, all of them located in what you

49

would call the mind of Harry Butler. However fast and however complicated a computer might be, it only thinks one thought at a time. Harry Butler's mind was like a room crowded with people all claiming to be Harry Butler, and each with interests and inclinations distinct from all the rest.

So one of the Harry Butlers was thinking he would like – and here I hesitated. I didn't want to shock Uta with too much frankness. Yet I couldn't really use her euphemism – "do something". So I said "have sex". He was thinking he would like to have sex with someone.

Uta wanted to know with whom. With Claire? Or with Louise?

I told her he didn't have anyone in particular in mind. It was just a vague sort of stirring in that part of his body. If he'd been asked he might even have said he would just like it to be with some nice woman who wouldn't give him any trouble with befores and afters.

Uta nodded, her mouth set tight. "This man could be a rapist," she said. "I recognize the type."

Erik looked impartial, and I thought he probably knew what I was talking about. So I pressed on.

Under or over this unfocussed sense of himself as a sexual animal Harry was doing the kind of thinking expected of a professor of philosophy. He was thinking about Mind and Body again, and the illustration was his own state of mind and body as he walked along. How could his thinking be disengaged from his physical sense of himself, his mood, a curious buoyancy so that he could feel the spring someone else might have seen in his stride, his awareness of the buzz of bees, the scent of flowers, and the assaults of a really very temperate current of air that seemed to rise cleanly from the harbour and sweep up at him over grass and trees? All of that, together with the anxieties, pushed well back but still present, that belonged to Arvon Crescent behind and to the university ahead. And finally, most mysteriously of all, his consciousness of all this activity in the very instant that it was happening, like an orchestra which was at once the players and the audience.

"So it was really much the same as his moment on the floor with his wife," Erik said. "But as a philosopher – what did he make of it?"

Here again I was uncertain, but I took a shot at speaking for Harry. "As a philosopher what could he make of it," I asked. "Maybe he was at the point where you go right through philosophy and come out the other side. It made him think again about language. The more you purified and purged language, pinned it down, the less of human consciousness it was able to carry."

The Consul looked puzzled. "So what follows from that?"

All I could tell them was what happened next. When Harry got to his office at the university his secretary, Edith, was ready to tell him he should do this and do that. But he made her wait while he typed something out in capital letters on a piece of paper. Then he stuck it up on a pin-board opposite his desk. It read THERE ARE ONLY PHILOSOPHICAL PROBLEMS AT THE POINT WHERE LANGUAGE BEGINS TO FAIL.

"I don't understand," Uta said.

The Consul was frowning. "It sounds like a rejection of philosophy."

"Possibly it was," I said.

TEN

An Unpleasant Scene

But that was only the beginning of Harry's day. Once the statement was typed out and put up on his pin-board there was nothing further that could hold Edith and her secretarial messages at bay. Already the Dean was waiting in the corridor with his complaint that Harry hadn't replied to his questions about the new Arts Faculty building, and that since Harry had also missed a crucial meeting of the Buildings Committee, everyone was in the dark about his Department's needs.

When the Dean had been dealt with there followed a pair, Midge and Les, from the Women's Collective, decidedly bra-less under their overalls, and complaining that preliminary plans for the new building showed no space, apart from lavatories, set aside exclusively for women. Harry said there were no spaces exclusively for men either, but that answer didn't satisfy them. So he made a note of their complaint and clipped it to the Dean's list of questions.

Louise Lamont came in without knocking just as the two from the Women's Collective were leaving. She said something like "Have you got a minute", and then without waiting for an answer she dropped into the nearest chair.

Or rather, not "into" the chair. She sat on its edge, facing the wall so Harry saw her side-on. Almost instantly there were tears in her eyes. As the door closed behind Les and Midge, Louise said "I can't stand it Harry."

It's important we see Louise as Harry saw her, because there's no arguing with some kinds of distress. They're real. Louise Lamont's distress was real.

So was Harry's. I've explained to Uta that I don't want to do any special pleading for Harry. She will probably say he brought all this on himself. Others might point out that Louise was old enough to take responsibility for her own actions. I leave all that aside. The ethics of it is not my business. My job is just to represent it as it happened.

So there were Louise's tears, and Harry's helplessness. The modern freewoman was in love again. Down had crashed all those defensive walls of intellect, precedent, and Women's Liberation. That, I suppose, was what distressed her, as much as the distress itself. This invasion of emotion, wanting someone, wanting more of a man than the man was able or willing to give – it was a state she'd resolved never to be in again.

As for Harry – it's difficult to avoid seeing him as someone who was losing control of his own life. Too many things were coming at him all at once. It made him confused and defensive. And he hated causing pain. Louise's tears upset him. What made it worse was that she was trying to control them – drying her cheeks with a handkerchief, doing something to her hair.

"It's O.K.," she said. "I'm just tense. I think my period's coming."

She was walking about the room now. She stopped at the window and looked down at the palms along the edge of the park. She crossed the room and looked at Harry's pin-board, and read the notice he'd typed out that morning: THERE ARE ONLY PHILOSOPHICAL

53

PROBLEMS AT THE POINT WHERE LANGUAGE BEGINS TO FAIL.

"That's good," she said. "I like it."

She read it again and then quoted the last sentence of Wittgenstein's *Tractatus*: "What we cannot speak about we must pass over in silence."

She went around behind Harry's chair and leaned over him, kissing him on the side of the neck, at the same time reaching down and putting her hand between his legs. There was an instant response down there, but he was aware the door wasn't locked and he didn't trust Edith not to come in without knocking. He began to say it – "The door . . . Edith might . . ."

"Oh fuck Edith," Louise said. But she took her hand away. "We've got to talk," she said.

Harry assented wearily. They had to talk. But he wished that what couldn't be spoken about might be passed over in silence.

She had gone back to her chair and she was staring at him.

"You've changed," she said. "These last few days – there's been a change."

He said he'd had his hair cut.

"I don't mean your hair. I mean you. I mean you in relation to me."

He shook his head. "I haven't changed. I'm just busy."

She went on staring at him. "You've fucked your wife," she said.

"Oh for God's sake," Harry said. "This is mad. Neurotic."

She looked unrepentant. He hadn't denied it. After another silence she said, "Let's go to the mountain."

"There's no snow."

"I wasn't thinking of skiing."

"You know I can't go away. What am I supposed to tell Claire?"

"I'm sorry. I forgot your wife has to be protected."

"Look, I don't want to go to the mountain. That lodge hasn't got the same sentimental appeal for me that it has for you."

"Oh Harry, how long are you going to go on throwing that up at me?"

Silence. He too looked as if he thought he was being unfair. After a moment she said "I'm faithful to you, Harry. I've been faithful for almost a year. And you're still living with your wife. Do you know what my friends would say if they knew?"

"I don't ask you to be faithful."

"No. You just suffer visibly if I'm not. And you keep dredging up that weekend I spent with Matthew. What am I supposed to do? I want to see more of you. I don't want to spend my time with other people."

She seemed to be on the brink of saying the thing he'd been able to rely on her pride as a modern liberated woman to prevent her from saying. She seemed to draw back from the brink. Then she stepped right over it.

"I want to be your wife. Why shouldn't I be? I'm your real wife now."

Harry's face took on a special kind of blankness. I don't think it was the blankness of concealment, the studied neutrality of the barrister or the cardsharp. It was more like the white-out effect you get when something is spun very fast. Inwardly Harry was spinning. As he came out of the spin he found himself talking about Ramadan, the Muslim holy month. He was explaining that since Claire had adopted her Sufi name, Sophia, she insisted they would have to observe Ramadan. That meant a month of

55

no eating during the hours of daylight. She had two threads of cotton hanging in the window, one black, one white. When it was too dark to distinguish between the black and the white the family would be allowed to eat. So during Ramadan they were going to get up before sunrise for breakfast – and that would be it. No more eating until it was dark again.

It wasn't quite clear even to Harry why he was telling Louise this. It was something embarrassing he'd kept concealed from his friends. Then, out of the thick of his confusion, Harry saw the logic.

"They need me," he said. "I mean the boys – Jonah and Reuben."

Louise sat silent, still staring at him. He said, "She spends hours sitting at that shrine chanting mantras at her whirling dervish."

Another silence. At last Louise said, "I don't believe you Harry."

He was wide-eyed with truth-telling. "It's true," he said. "She's gone right overboard . . ."

Louise cut across him. "It's not the boys. It's Claire."

He shook his head but he didn't answer.

"You love her," Louise said. "You've never stopped loving her."

He went on staring at his hands as if he expected them to do something. It was obvious she believed what she said and didn't expect him to deny it, but she must have been hoping that he would. His silence only confirmed what she meant – that after the first excitement of their affair his emotions had settled back into their old pattern. Claire was still the centre of his existence. It was as if that spinning disk had lost its white-out blankness. It had run down, tottered, toppled sideways and stopped, and there,

56

written clearly on its face, was the single word "No".

Louise stood up. She must have felt ill-used and angry. "I don't mind if that's what you feel, Harry. But I hate it that you lie to me and confuse me."

"I don't lie to you."

"Well if you don't lie you don't tell me the truth. Not the whole truth."

"I don't know what the whole truth is. It shifts. It's like the weather. What am I supposed to give you? Regular reports?"

"You tell me what suits you. You want to keep me in just the right place – not too close and not too far away."

"I don't lie to you," he repeated. "If I'm ever guilty of not telling you the whole truth it's because I don't want to hurt you."

She stood very still for a moment. "That's getting nearer," she said. "The truth would hurt so you don't tell it."

He shook his head. "You're confusing me."

"The truth is you don't love me."

"The truth is I do."

"But you're not going to leave your vegetarian wife. Well, that's O.K. I never asked you to or expected you to. Maybe I'd like it if it happened. It's true I think about it sometimes. But it's just day-dreaming. I know that."

He wanted to comfort her, to tell her it wasn't just day-dreaming. But he couldn't. He remained silent, staring at his useless hands.

"You want to be rid of me," she said.

"I don't want that at all. But I'd like to be rid of the guilt. It's all in my favour. It's all arranged to suit me. You should have other friends. I mean . . ." His voice tailed away.

"You mean another lover don't you. And if I do you'll go around looking like a stuck pig."

"Probably. At least I'll know I'm not stopping you leading a normal life."

"Isn't it up to me to decide whether I want what you call a normal life? I'm not a child. You don't have to protect me."

He looked up at her. "I'm not sure about that. I feel protective."

She shook her head. "You want everything Harry. All the pleasure. No trouble. And no guilt." She sat down again on the edge of her chair. "What would Claire do if I went and told her about us?"

It has to be said that Harry was good in a crisis, especially if there was the suggestion of a threat. His face went blank again, and this time it probably was the studied blankness of the barrister or the cardsharp. "I don't know," he said. "She might invite you in to join her on the prayer-mat. Or she might have some secret Sufi method for disposing of the enemies of truth."

Silence again, until he said, "You can't force it, Louise. If you want to take revenge on me you can do that any time. But you can't force it. It just has to take its course."

"I don't want to force it. And I don't want to take revenge. And I couldn't if I wanted to. You know you're safe Harry."

He shook his head. He didn't feel safe.

Louise said, "You know what those two who were in here a moment ago would say, don't you? The two from the Women's Collective. They'd say you know you're safe because I'm still your student and I need your good opinion. I need it on paper. If I don't have it I don't have a future."

Harry was shocked. "You don't believe that do you? If I write a reference for you it has nothing to do with your personal life or mine."

"Stop pretending you're not human," she said.

"I'm not pretending anything. A reference is about your academic record and your research work . . ."

"And my personality. Don't be naive Harry. If you wrote me a reference today it would be a better one than I deserve because we've been lovers. And because you feel guilty about me. If I went around to Mission Bay and put a bomb under your marriage it wouldn't be as good as I deserve . . ."

Harry stood up. He was suddenly angry. "Fuck off then," he said. "Tell the Women's Collective I'm guilty of sexual harassment because I won't marry you. And shut the door as you go out."

But she didn't go. She sat on the edge of that chair, side-on to Harry, facing the wall. Once again there were those tears. No sobs. Just tears. And silence.

Harry tried not to look. He preferred himself as the fighter. There was less pain. At last she dried her eyes and got up. She walked slowly to the door. Watching him from back here behind the lights in my mental film studio I feel like shouting at him to say something, to follow her to the door, to take her in his arms, but he doesn't move. He stands there like some iron-plated Coriolanus winning another famous victory to Rome. It all seems to happen very slowly. Probably he doesn't want her to leave without another word. But if there's going to be another word it will have to come from her. And of course it does. There's a long pause at the door and then she says "Harry" and turns around and comes back. He rubs the back of her neck and kisses her ear.

"I have to have some weapons," she says. "I can't be totally helpless like this."

He mumbles his assent. In fact it all dissolves now into mumbles and caresses, through which it might just be possible to make out that Harry is telling her she has to choose her weapon if that's how she feels, and be ready to use it. Whether he means it or not can't be clear, even to himself. And it's obvious it isn't a weapon she wants. She wants Harry.

Not an edifying scene, and not one I relish putting before Uta Haverstrom; but as I've explained, she has become some kind of monitor, or arbiter – I'm not sure how or why but it's so and I will have to show it to her.

And it doesn't end with a ringing line or a witty one. It ends with mumbles and fumbles and the door opening as Edith enters with a slip of paper in her hand and a look of prim urgency on her face. No one seems able to think of anything to say. Edith retreats, Harry and Louise disentangle themselves, and a moment later Harry is alone, staring once again at the pin-board and trying to recover what it was he meant by the statement that there were only philosophical problems at the point where language began to fail.

ELEVEN

Waiting for Jason

Down in the little café on the Corso Magenta the padrone and the Consul's wife sometimes argue with me about how the story should be told. The other morning Uta said I was a man of sensibility, of intelligence and finer feelings, and that I should put them on display. I was grateful for the tribute of course, although I wasn't quite sure she meant what she said; but I told her my feelings had nothing to do with it. My job was to get it down exactly as it happened. She told me I was in danger of writing something "heartless". I think she had in mind the scene between Harry Butler and Louise Lamont. I tried to explain to her that I'm not in control. Or rather, that I'm in control but not in charge. I wondered whether I should explain about the voice from the blue folder but I decided against it. I think she would have found it either insane or merely whimsical. Uta is a very literal-minded woman. I conceded that Harry was rough on Louise in that scene, but I pointed out that he was under all kinds of pressure – and the padrone nodded in agreement. "Is hard life that Harry prof," he said, making one of his shots at a statement in English.

Uta frowned and shook her head. "You men," she said. "You stick up for one another. When will women learn to do the same?"

I like Uta and I'm glad of her presence in the café, but

these conversations sometimes go on too long. I've noticed lately that I drink more coffee and write fewer pages. That's why the Story and ' are taking a brief trip to Turin. We travel by rail, first class on a single ticket. It's winter now, and we have the compartment to ourselves. Today the fogs have cleared, the sky is blue, and we race along looking at snow-covered mountains across fields whose brown furrows look stiff with frost. The Story lies on the seat beside me in its blue folder. Travel makes it talkative while the rhythm of the train at high speed makes me drowsy. I go into a sort of half-sleep, dreaming (I have to admit) of slim blonde Uta uncovering a wonderfully full sweater as she takes off her heavy coat at the door of the café. At the same time I seem to hear the Story, talking now to that line of mountains crystal-clear against a winter sky. I think it's complaining about me – about my tendency to interfere. And it doesn't seem to like Uta, especially when she claims to speak for the human heart, which the Story regards as an inferior recording instrument, not to be compared with the camera (a Pentax K2) of John Sprott. I must indeed be dreaming because in this dialogue I hear the mountains agree, and I comment that this is no surprise since they seem to exist only to be photographed.

In my account of Harry's walk to the university on the morning when he was visited by Louise Lamont, I said it could have been before or after he sent the drug squad packing. But the Story insists there's no either/or. It must have been after. We argue about this, but I have to concede the Story's right. To explain why I will have to track back a little.

When Edith came in without knocking (or, as in her version of what happened, her knock wasn't heard) and found Harry and Louise wrapped around one another, what she came to say was that she'd managed to get a message through to Jason Cook. It was one of the things Harry had asked her to do after he'd typed out his sentence in capitals and pinned it up on his board. Harry's message was that he would be in the Turf Bar of the Hotel Intercontinental around 5 that evening with Phil, and he especially hoped Jason would join them. Edith came in with the report that she'd got through to Jason and that he would be there but that he might be late.

Harry's reason for wanting to see Jason was to tell him how close he'd come to getting his face into drug squad files, and to ask him what he'd been doing visiting number 27 Arvon Crescent. That's why I have to concede that the Story is right. Because it was Harry getting in the way of the drug squad camera that precipitated the angry exchange which ended in him asking them to leave. And that in turn means that the scene with Louise Lamont must have occurred after, not before.

So I have after all brought us back to the scene we began with. In fact I've taken us right past it. We'll return to it later if that should prove necessary.

We have now to consider once again the three, Harry, Phil and Jason, who had been at the same school and who remained friends. We last saw them together, a brief glance contained I think in a single sentence or camera shot, at Phil Gardner's wedding after his return from London, where Jason met for the first time Harry's first wife, Natalie. There they are, preserved in Kiri Gardner's photograph album, three men and two women, arms linked, on a well-mown lawn with what looks like a lilac tree in full flower behind them. They're doing some kind of dance – each has one leg crossed over in front of the other and they're laughing and squinting into the sun. Harry and Phil are on either end, and Jason, a tall elegant figure in a suit exactly matching the other two, in the centre. Between Jason and Harry is the bride, Kiri; and between Jason and Phil is Natalie. As if to predict her elimination from the group, one of those swirls of light that get into old snapshots has partly concealed, or at least made less distinct, Natalie's face, so it isn't possible to see what a beautiful young woman she was.

Turning the pages of that same album you would almost certainly come on the shot of Natalie dancing in the shallows of the West Coast surf (true Frenchwoman she never actually plunged in and swam) waving her arms about; and the one of her on the dunes, arms spread wide, head back, with the wind dragging her hair out behind her.

A page or two on come shots of a lunch party Jason gave when he bought a small house up on a cliff overlooking one of the bays north of Milford. The view from the front of the house looks down the Hauraki Gulf towards Rangitoto. And there are shots of the view the other way, looking over the heads of pohutukawas and toi toi and flax down to the little bay and the still water, beyond which the next cliff rises with matching vegetation. In these you can see it's the colours that enticed Kiri to repeat more or less the same shot again and again – red pohutukawa flowers (it must have been December), the dark shiny green of its leaves and of the flax, the blowsy white of what's left of the toi toi heads, the yellow sand and the blue-green water of the bay. On the lawn in front of the house, eating chicken legs and salad and bread and drinking white wine, are variously Natalie and Harry, Jason and Phil, Phil and Kiri, and some other people, names now forgotten. There's even a shot of the ramshackle shed around the back of the house where Jason stored the cheap detergent he was just beginning to sell in bulk to restaurants and cafeterias. Jason had given up working as a trainer of trotting horses; and those were the days when people started up small businesses and made a profit out of them.

There was a lot Harry and Phil didn't know about Jason. For example what became of the sherry-drinking mother with shares in South African diamond mines? She was never spoken about now. And what about the big house in Remuera whose hedge the three boys did or didn't set on fire? Then there was the question of whether Jason had or hadn't been briefly married while the other two were abroad. It had never been mentioned in letters, nor in conversation after their return. But Claire had met a woman, the wife of a city councillor, who said to her at a cocktail party "I think your husband is a friend of my first husband, Jason Cook." When this was mentioned Jason's face took on a neutral expression and he told them not to believe everything they heard at cocktail parties.

While Phil and Harry waited that evening for Jason to turn up, sitting in a quiet corner of the Turf Bar of what was still then called the Hotel Intercontinental (like Claire Butler and the chinese gooseberry it too was about to have a change of name), Harry had time to spill the beans about his problems. This wasn't unusual. Phil had listened to a lot of confessions at the time when Natalie was leaving the scene and Claire was entering. And now in the past year he'd had to absorb the fact of Louise Lamont. He hadn't met Louise and he had no wish to. He thought of her as something voluptuous in soft focus – one of those girls in magazines like *Playboy* or *Penthouse* which he allowed himself to glance at in airport bookshops but never bought. Or as a girl in a James Bond movie in glossy red and black against a brilliant white ski-slope – the kind you can write out of the script by turning her into an enemy agent immediately after the sex scene in front of the log fire in the mountain chalet.

Phil didn't really approve of the irregularities in Harry's sex life, but he accepted them. They were Harry, and Harry was an old friend. And they interested him. He was a good listener when Harry needed to talk.

So Phil heard about the scene with Louise Lamont. He shook his head. He told Harry he was taking risks. He worried about Edith coming in on them like that. And what about those two from the Women's Collective? It wasn't the first time Phil had criticized Harry for being passive and letting things happen to him instead of taking charge of his own life.

Mixed up with their conversation about Louise there was the subject of the drug squad and Jason's appearance on the drive of number 27 Arvon Crescent, and Harry's pretence at a tantrum which had finally got Larson Snow and John Sprott out of his house. This was a subject that interested Phil as a journalist. He'd written articles for his paper about the Mr Asia Syndicate, and the trial of Alexander Sinclair, and the Australian Royal Commission on drugs. Again he warned Harry that he was taking risks.

During the last part of my journey to Turin I wake up and think seriously about all this. It's on my mind as I walk through the streets to my hotel, which is near the station. Was Harry Butler really a reckless person, given to living dangerously? I don't think he was at all. You might say he was impulsive; but the impulses fitted into a tight framework that never varied. Even Louise Lamont had to accommodate herself to that framework. That was why she'd come to his office to tell him she couldn't stand it any longer.

When I reach my hotel I find there's a message asking me to call Uta at the Milan consulate as soon as I get in. I can't imagine what might have happened that requires an urgent phone call; and when I get through to her it's only that she has been thinking very hard about Harry and decided that he isn't serious about Louise. He's using her for his own pleasure, as a sex object. But Uta has decided Harry doesn't love Claire either. There's something cold and unyielding about him, she says, which goes along with his being a professor of philosophy. Some essential humanity has withered in him. And she thinks I should make this fact (she calls it a fact) quite clear.

I conceal my irritation and thank her once again for her interest.

"And wear your overcoat when you go out," she says. "It's going to be a cold night."

As usual Uta sets up in me a strange agitation. I'm angry, and yet I'm glad of her call. I go out again (taking my overcoat as instructed) and walk about the city, admiring and yet feeling oppressed by the military precision with which its huge squares and arcades have been laid out. Finally I retire to a little place recommended by Uta called the Trattoria di Betty. I take the blue folder with me, and after a meal of vegetable soup and green pasta, I settle down to work. Is Harry an exploiter of women's feelings? Or is he a victim of his own? Is he a heartless man, or a man with too much heart?

The Story and I don't think it's our job to answer such questions, even supposing there are answers to be given. It's a rare moment of accord between us. So I write a quick

67

postcard to Uta telling her I am wearing my overcoat and that the Trattoria di Betty is as good as she said it was. And then I return to my scene – Harry and Phil talking in that quiet corner of the Turf Bar, still waiting for Jason.

By now Harry has resolved not to be passive, not to let life roll over him. He will write a letter to Louise suggesting they shouldn't see one another for a while – maybe a month, or six weeks. That will give her time to sort herself out, achieve some sort of detachment, maybe find herself a new lover – someone nearer to her own age. He won't say all this in the letter. He'll just give some good general reasons why a cooling-off period seems to be called for.

Harry has been quite sincere, even enthusiastic, probably because it means one of the pressures will be removed from his life. But Phil, who has been encouraging him, notices him beginning to hesitate at the thought that Louise will probably find herself another man.

It has to be mentioned that Jason has kept them waiting a long time, so Harry has had quite a lot to drink. All at once he goes off at a tangent and begins to complain about Claire's Sufism. He says he married a beautiful intelligent woman and that Duag MacPherson is turning her into a mantra-chanting coathanger. He says he ought to go around and beat the shit out of the carpet seller.

The anger is sudden and violent, and it crosses Phil's mind that Harry is probably jealous of Duag MacPherson and the power he exerts over Claire.

"Divest yourself of the love of created things," Harry quotes. "That's what she's learning from that third rate witchdoctor. Detachment. You know why? I think she wants to fuck God. Well she can fuck God. I'll fuck Louise."

68

Phil too has had a lot to drink and he's running out of patience. "Bloody snakes and ladders," he says. "Up the ladder, down the snake. Where's Jason?"

And it's just at that moment that Jason walks in. He's dressed in boots, blue jeans, a blue check shirt, with a red cotton scarf tied in a knot at his throat. He looks fit and tanned – positive and full of energy.

"Sorry I'm late, chaps," he says. "Unavoidable detention. My round. What's it to be? I'm in the money."

They tell him what they're drinking and watch as he pushes his way to the bar.

Harry wipes a hand wearily over his eyes. "Bugger's in the money," he says. "I was afraid of that."

TWELVE

Harry by Night

Mind/Body. Body/Mind. If Body urges you one way and Mind another, doesn't that make you a third person? But which way were they urging Harry Butler?

Imagine him roaming from room to room in the dark house. He looks into Jonah's bedroom, then into Reuben's. He straightens their bedclothes in the half light. He looks into their faces. He walks into the little shrine room, where the Body/Mind book was to have been written, watched over now by the clay figurine of the whirling dervish. He thinks of Claire's mantra, and his, and what they did there on the floor. He goes to the window and looks out. He wonders what Louise is doing, and resists the temptation to call her. He goes to the bedroom door and hears Claire breathing evenly in the dark. He goes out on to the front verandah and looks down at the lights on the water at the harbour entrance.

We've gone back a day or so. Harry has yet to push his grey-striped shirt in front of the Pentax K2. The drug squad haven't been thrown out. But at night they leave the house. Do they set up some alternative watching post? Or is Greg Carey allowed free passage between 11 p.m. and 8 a.m.? If he is, he makes good use of it. His sports car is up and down the drive often during those hours. There he goes now, and for a moment Mandy looks out between the curtains, watching him. From the dark of the kitchen

Harry watches her watching Greg. Mandy scratching her arms. Mandy of the beautiful pin-point eyes, staring at herself in the mirror. Narcissus, shutting out the world.

Observation, Harry thinks. Looking at things, noticing them, watching the cat washing itself. Watching it stare and blink and look away. Observing the pattern of moonlight on the lassiandra leaves. Escape. Escape out of the head, and out of the mirror. Are he and Mandy two of a kind?

It's in this silence that his feelings seem clearest to him. If he thinks of Mandy, he loves her. When he hears Claire breathing it's the same. It washes over him. The telephone sitting there by the window is a line to Louise – and again, a surge of feeling. In the two little bedrooms he puts his hand on his sons'' heads, Jonah, then Reuben. It's like testing yourself for a response. The dry, stiff, probably muddy hair on their sleeping heads does it again. Another flood of affection.

Harry goes back to the window. Greg Carey's sports has come back into the drive. He can't have gone far. Did he see something up the road? Did they put a tail on him? Are the RTs crackling "He's gone back, boss. I think he saw us"?

Today the squad were in the big house next door. In there swiftly and silently – it was impressive. Some time between five and six in the afternoon. Greg and Mandy off together somewhere in the sports. Larson Snow putting a tail on them and monitoring it on the RT. They were driving towards Royal Oak, then veering off left towards Penrose, travelling south. Larson decided they were far enough away. Everything was ready. In minutes there was a whole team of them in overalls looking like electricians, or plumbers, or (Harry thought) the Women's Collective, but with a dog. They went into the house without breaking anything, hardly moving anything, but they trusted their dog. If there were drugs in there he would find them. If they were hidden behind wall-panelling, or under floorboards, he would nose them out. Even buried on the lawn or in the flower beds they would be found. They went through every room in the house. Nothing. Long before the tail reported on the RT that the sports had turned for home, they'd withdrawn. Larson was satisfied. He didn't doubt Greg Carey was trading, but the goods must be kept somewhere else. So nothing more. No occasion for it. It was no use blowing the place apart and blowing your cover if there was nothing to be found except a few roaches, and no conviction to be had. When he puts Greg Carey away Larson wants it to be for ten years.

But if the dog would sniff the goods out from under floor boards or behind panelling, what about up on the roof? Harry asks himself this now because the dark figure of Greg has parked the sports and gone indoors, re-emerged on the balcony, and now he's going like Jack up the beanstalk on to the roof. The beanstalk in this case is that huge chinese gooseberry vine which these days travels internationally as a kiwi fruit. The roof is flat. Greg is up the vine and on to it, silhouetted against the sky for a few minutes, crouching over something among the leaves (a plastic container? Something to keep the rain out?) and then he's down again, quickly. There must be a supply somewhere not far away – he was gone in the sports such a short time. And the roof is a kind of holding depot.

Now they've pulled the gauzy curtain across the bedroom's plate glass. Harry can see the two of them in cloudy outline. Greg, a long thin black shadow, has thrown himself down on the bed, on his back, still

72

dressed. One movement of the arm suggests he's smoking. Mandy has gone to the mirror. She doesn't go there in the daytime any more, when the curtains are open. That's the only sign there has been that she might have heard Harry's whispered warning beside the clothes line.

Through the gauze Harry can see Mandy undressing in front of the mirror, watching herself, doing a kind of dance of the seven veils. Greg's head remains on the pillow, his hand bringing the cigarette to his lips and away to an ashtray somewhere. She's watching herself. He's not watching anything. He's locked inside his head, probably counting money.

Harry imagines what might be passing between them – Mandy, willowy in front of the mirror, singing "Chama-chama-chama-chama-chama-chameleon, you come and go, come and go-o-o-o", in her husky-high, silly-silky and (to Harry) lovely voice. The hips waver and undulate. He's had his hands on those hips when they were moving like that. He remembers the rough texture of the silver dress she was wearing, and her hair tickling his ear as she leaned towards him, singing that song.

Greg lies there, long, dark, invertebrate, not looking at her swaying and dancing. She's either naked now or down to pale underwear.

On his imaginary bug Harry hears Greg: "Stop looking at yourself", and her reply, "No one else looks at me. So I look at myself."

Would she say that? Or would she say "Fuck off" as she did at the clothes line? Or would she just go on singing "Chama-chama-chama-chama-chama-chameleon, you come and go, come and go-o-o-o"?

She's dancing towards the bed now, her arms over her head, throwing away maybe the last of the wispy seven

73

veils, bought probably in Hong Kong or Bali or Singapore – closing on her cut-out man with her pin-point eyes.

"Stop pretending you're sexy," Greg says.

Harry imagines it and winces. Would Greg say that? Probably. Something, anyway, has stopped her in her tracks. The willowy dance in his direction is finished. She stands a moment, quite still, then pulls on a dressing gown. Now she's out on the balcony, staring down over the house-roofs towards the sea. Sulking. The man in black still lies stretched out on the bed, finishing his cigarette.

Why hasn't Mandy passed on Harry's warning to Greg? Because she doesn't care? Because she wants her world blown apart and can't do it herself? Or maybe just for the simpler reason that she would have to explain to Greg that she knows Harry, and how and where they met.

There are a lot of things Harry would like to ask her. It seems strange to be staring at her across the shadowy divide of his own back lawn and garden. Gatsbyish. But also frightening.

Greg has got up from the bed. He's shedding his black clothes, no longer cardboard, becoming a white blur, probably naked. Now he gets into bed. The light goes out. The figure of Mandy is still out there on the balcony, staring down towards the sea, from which comes a mild early summer breeze. She turns indoors, into the bedroom. The light doesn't go on again. Now she must be getting into the big bed with Greg.

Harry tries to imagine them in there. Making love? He doesn't think so. He imagines an exchange of complaints and minor accusations. Or maybe just silence. But not the silence of sleep. They lead such static lives, waiting for something to happen.

Or maybe Greg sleeps, Mandy lying awake staring at the ceiling, imagining herself in the mirror. Singing to herself in that high, soft, now-and-then just off-the-note voice.

Harry goes out of doors. He picks a lemon off the tree, walking out to the gate. A figure in a leather jacket moving away from the gate of number 27 hesitates, stops. "Nice night prof." It's Larson Snow. "Just passing so I thought I'd throw a glance around."

If he'd come ten minutes earlier he might have seen Greg Carey go up on to the roof. The cat up there has lost another of his nine lives. He has been lucky, but he doesn't know it.

"I think they've gone to bed," Harry says.

"Even dealers have to sleep."

"You're still convinced he deals."

Larson Snow laughs quietly in the dark, lighting a cigarette. "You got a better idea?"

"I try not to think about it," Harry says.

THIRTEEN

Mind and Body, Head and Heart

A day or so after I got back to Milan I went to the Café Corso Magenta at the usual time and found Uta already waiting for me. She seemed agitated, almost irritable. She didn't like the scene in which Harry moons about feeling surges of love for three women and two sons.

"To be frank with you," she said frankly, "I don't believe it."

I assured her it was true – Harry was like that – but she said she was sure she knew his type and that I wasn't telling the whole truth about him.

The padrone, who was still clearing up from the previous night, intervened. He didn't like to see us quarrel. Hadn't she complained (he reminded her) that the story was heartless? Now that it had some heart, was she going to complain again?

Uta replied that she didn't want to see Harry's heart (his false heart, she called it). She wanted to see the broken hearts of his women. She wanted the truth to be told.

"You don't want heart," I told her. "You want morals."

The toss of her head and the silence which followed suggested that was the end of it. We would discuss it no further. I was tempted to leave it there. But I couldn't. In some way I couldn't explain I felt bound to Uta. I had to argue it out with her. So I asked her to be more specific in her complaints. What was it she needed to know about Harry Butler?

She gave it some thought. "You must tell me more about his relations with Claire" was what she finally came out with.

This was something which I suppose unconsciously I'd hoped to avoid. Not because there was anything to hide, but because it was difficult, and I didn't feel as if I understood it perfectly. Harry's anger in the Turf Bar had made him exaggerate when he said Duag MacPherson was turning Claire from a beautiful woman into a mantra-chanting coathanger. But still there was just enough truth in it to make anyone who thought about it ask why.

Harry was in the habit of saying that in human affairs there were no causes, only facts and circumstances. But we all – even Harry – look for causes. We all ask "Why?" And so I had to accept it was reasonable for Uta to ask it.

I tried to focus on Claire as she'd been when Harry first knew her, and the image that came to mind was of a small, neat 21-year-old in red tights and a leather mini-skirt. Possibly the shirt already had some Indian embroidery; and over the shirt there might have been a sleeveless leather jerkin.

Once I'd put that image together it didn't seem right. I wanted to convey that Claire had a lot of clothes and that she dressed with flair.

The cool blue eyes of Uta Haverstrom looked at me across the table, waiting. I don't suppose the red tights and the leather mini-skirt impressed her, but she let that pass. She must have known well enough about the fashions of that time. She might have worn them herself when she was a student. Or would she have been too conservative? But none of this was said. She simply looked at me and

77

waited. What was she to make of the fact that Claire wore interesting clothes?

The padrone came to my rescue again. Maybe he remembered how he'd asked me, when I'd been telling him about Natalie, to give him a scene. He asked it again. A scene, Maestro Balzac (he liked to repeat his joke) if you please. Something for his late-night screen when the place went quiet and there were only one or two couples whispering over the table tops.

But my mind seemed empty. I could think of nothing. No use asking the Story. It wouldn't co-operate in this kind of cross-examination. Probably it was keen to move forward.

And then out of the blankness up it came – a scene, two characters, dialogue. Even at the time, Claire had seen it as something out of an American campus movie because Harry was wearing a pale jacket, and in her mind, which in those days had a constant half-turn towards comedy, she converted his knotted woven tie into a bow tie and imagined him as an American professor. You have to picture him standing on the verandah of her flat in Ponsonby. Uneven flooring, unpainted weatherboards, coloured glass door panels, finials where the gables peak – we all know the house a dozen times over. It's always scheduled for demolition because a motorway is to go through or a town house to be built.

Harry has driven her home. Already they know one another quite well. There's a lot of eager feeling between them – but undeclared, unfocused. The air quivers with it. Whatever the weather was in "reality", in the mind and (Yes, dear heartless Uta) in the heart – not to mention in the padrone's movie – it's going to have to be crystal clear, still, moonlit, every twig, every grassblade clean-edged and sharp to the eye.

They've sat talking in the front seat of the car. Now she wants to show him a poem by Wordsworth (she's a student of English, studying the Romantic poets). He goes in with her and sees her bedroom, which strikes him as something like a changing room at the Old Vic might look. She shows him the poem. He reads it and they talk about it.

Now they're out on that verandah, and still what must be obvious to both remains unspoken. Not that they're silent. They talk so easily their talk runs across the silences that might otherwise precipitate a declaration.

Claire looks if anything younger than her 21 years. Harry in the linen jacket looks anxious, harassed, but still youthful to be the professor he has recently become. And in her eyes at least, his thin, over-stretched look has something heroic about it. You can see that life isn't easy for him; and you can see he doesn't think it should be.

Natalie is on her way back to France. She and Harry have pretended to the world, and even to one another, that it's just a visit, that she will be back. Neither of them believes it, but they can't quite face, or admit to, their own disbelief. Natalie will love "ze sous seas" much better from a café in Paris. There she will be able to draw over them once again their atmosphere of Gallic romance. She will remember Harry affectionately and say her first marriage didn't work out because she was too young to know what she was doing.

But Harry hasn't been talking to Claire about Natalie. As far as Claire knows Harry is Professor Butler, a married man with a striking and stylish French wife. And as far as Harry has admitted to himself, this is still the case.

79

Their talk, his and Claire's, has been about philosophy, and Wordsworth, and music. She wants to play him a record by Lou Reed and the Velvet Underground, but she's afraid at this hour they might wake the couple upstairs. So he has at least an excuse for returning.

Now, standing out on the verandah, and with the talk working on him a little like alcohol, he's admitting that at the age of thirty-three, and having just been elevated to the new professorship, he feels old, and finished as a philosopher. Ideas used to come to him more or less out of the air. Not all the time. But they came, and they were fresh and original. Gilt-edged. Gift-wrapped. Now he has to force himself. Thinking hard, thinking deliberately, he finds himself slow, laborious, unoriginal, uninspired. In his lectures he's beginning to repeat himself, going through old examples which seem to him like dead fish that have lost the sparkle and colour they had when they first came out of the water. He tells her how he forces himself with a problem, becoming so obsessed with it he has to go to a movie to switch his mind off.

She tells him Wordsworth had a mental breakdown through forcing his mind like that. She tells him he should learn meditation. She suggests some movies he should see. Hers are French movies. He admits to a preference for Hollywood Westerns and thrillers. She tells him when he feels like that he should visit her. She will play him the Lou Reed record. Or she might even play the guitar herself and sing some protest ballads.

That seems to be the end of it. Have they both given up on a declaration? Harry turns to go, then turns back. He says "Let me kiss you goodnight."

Where does the camera go now? Not on the kiss, or hardly for more than a moment. All kisses are alike from

80

the outside. To catch the inner essence of this one you would have to send your lens off in search of stars. Or let it move in so close to its subject it blacks out altogether. When we can see again we're back indoors, this time in Claire's little kitchen. She has put the kettle on. She sinks into a stiff-backed wooden chair, as if her legs won't hold her any longer. "What are we going to do," is what she says.

Harry says "I'd like to go to bed with you," and she laughs, as if to say that's the least of their problems.

Not a lot more is said after Harry's ("predictable", Uta calls it) mention of bed, and Claire's laugh. There's the sound of the gas jet under the kettle; there's the stark light over them in the primitive little student kitchen with linoleum on the floor; and outside the window, the dark branches of the wilderness that has grown up where a motorway is to be built.

On Claire's face a smile still lingers from the laugh. It's an inward expression of her sense of cosmic comedy, as in imagination she replaces the knot of woven cloth at her new lover's professorial throat with a little red bow tie with polka dots.

He looks strained beyond endurance. He's sitting on a stool, leaning towards her, elbows on knees, and now he lets his head drop forward on her lap. She lifts it as if it's disconnected from his body and cradles it in her arms. The philosopher's head. She smiles to herself, hugging it gently, kissing its ears. "Harry Butler," she says . . .

I had to cut the scene there. I needed to use the padrone's gabinetto, but in fact it was the right place to make a break. When I came back the padrone and Uta were disagreeing about Harry. She found his constant insistence on sex insensitive and boring. The padrone, northern Italian though he was, was more accepting. He shook his head. It might be deplorable, he told her, but it was normal.

But it wasn't sex that had brought Harry and Claire together. I tried to explain this, in English because it was difficult. Uta translated for the padrone, and that at least kept her from interrupting me.

Of course Harry and Claire were lovers quite soon. Probably there were the usual hesitations and adjustments, common enough when people change partners, but there was no need to go into that, was there? (Nordic head was shaken, Latin shoulders were lifted.)

So there was sex, which in itself is something like a mechanical event. When they got the mechanics sorted out, when they were making one another happy, what else was there? It's what goes along with the mechanics, and before them and after, that makes the difference. It's heads that make bodies sexy, and Harry and Claire in their different ways possessed exceptional heads.

So our movie might show a bed like a landscape after a hurricane. It's not going to show you the hurricane. Why shouldn't it (for example) track from the unmade bed to the corner in which Claire sits plucking at her guitar strings and singing. And from there to Harry on the couch, listening, his head hanging over the edge, almost touching the floor, his eyes on the light reflected off her fish tank on to the ceiling. Stillness – and out there the branches, moving just faintly.

Or the two might be seen walking on an empty beach north of Auckland, and she's telling him very earnestly, as if the detail of it matters, something, anything at all, an incident, a fear, a pleasure, out of her childhood.

There's a danger with these montage effects, scene laid

over scene, of sentimentality, I suppose. The touch needs to be light.

But how could you convey the substance of those letters of Claire's written in black ink? You couldn't. They spoke (I told Uta) straight from the heart. But without the head the heart would have had no voice. And without the head of Harry Butler to appreciate their special quality, down to the subtlest turn of phrase, what the heart was saying, and how truthfully, would have gone unregistered. "Don't", I told Uta, "accuse Harry Butler of being interested only in sex. If you believe that" (and as I said it I felt I was taking an awful risk) "you might as well go back to the Consul and help him with the morning mail."

Uta seemed to make a concession here, but really it was only a change of tack. O.K. she would accept that Harry loved Claire, that Claire loved Harry. Even, if I insisted on it, she would accept that their love was exceptional. She would let me off the sequence of scenes it would need to construct that love in convincing detail. She could build it up for herself. She was not (she assured me) inexperienced in these matters. So suppose we took for granted Harry's passion, and his sincerity. Natalie had gone and wouldn't return, and the reasons for that had been given. Harry was free to fall in love again. He had no special obligations. All this Uta accepted. She would even let me off the awkward question of what happened to Claire's boyfriend.

But having made these concessions Uta now turned them against me – or rather, against Harry. So he loved this young woman Claire. So he married her and she bore him two children. What was he now doing having an affair with Louise Lamont? When I'd answered that one, she said, she would have some supplementary questions concerning his as yet unexplained interest in the drug-dealer's girlfriend next door.

And as I opened my mouth to make some sort of stab at a reply she cut across me, forestalling what she thought might be the excuse I would make for Harry. "Don't tell me it's because Claire became a Sufi," she said. "Or because she turned against sex. If it had been a good marriage that wouldn't have happened."

But I hadn't been about to say either of those things. What had been hovering in my mind was that formula of Harry's: "In human affairs there are no causes, only facts and circumstances." Uta's persistence was driving me into a corner where what was true in the formula became clearer to me. It was the same corner occupied by the Story, which wanted only to press on.

I'm sure the blue folder was amused at the tangle I'd got myself into with the Consul's wife. But it warned me too. It, and not I, would decide when any supplementary questions (as Uta called them) were to be answered.

I asked for another coffee and the padrone got up to make it. He looked at me over the top of the espresso machine with sad, amused Italian eyes. "Maybe Maestro you're the wrong person to be telling this story. Maybe it should be told by a modern woman who wouldn't make excuses for the professor."

That pleased Uta of course. But it also cleared my head. I didn't want to make excuses for Harry or for anyone. I just wanted to see things as they had been. Of course I agreed something must have gone wrong between Harry and Claire. If the beginning had been so wonderful it ought to have gone on at least reasonably well.

And when I sought for an image, something precise to focus on that might help to explain the change, what I came back to was that very scene I thought we'd finished with, the one in Claire's kitchen while the gas jet hissed under the kettle, and Harry's head fell forward on her lap. It was the head of Harry Butler that Claire took in her arms, almost as if it didn't belong to his body. And his flat – even crass, if you want to see it as Uta did – statement "I'd like to go to bed with you" was turned aside with a laugh. Had Harry always been first and foremost a head to Claire? Even a professorial head? And hadn't his intellectual effort been directed always towards solving the Mind/Body paradox by saying the separation was unreal?

When Louise Lamont leaned over the back of his chair and cupped her hands around the package between his legs, was she further from Harry's head than Claire was with his head cradled in her arms? Or was she nearer?

It was a fine point of definition I'd come to, and I knew that I'd left Uta Haverstrom unsatisfied, even angry. What I seemed to be suggesting was that it was Claire, not professorial Harry, who lived too much in the head.

Uta didn't bother to argue. She simply turned it against me, and left me without an answer. If Claire lived too much in the head, she asked, why did Harry not teach her how to live in the body?

FOURTEEN

Down by the Shark Aquarium

Down on the Waterfront Drive where the old sewage tanks under the road were being converted into a shark aquarium Detective-Sergeant Larson Snow and Constable John Sprott of the Auckland police drug squad were meeting Phil Gardner, special features editor of an Auckland newspaper.

The handshake and the exchange of greeting signalled the tone they were going to maintain – a sort of clipped, no-nonsense, man-of-the-world style. These two, Larson and Phil, knew one another. Their work overlapped. Phil wrote sometimes about the drug squad's operations, and Larson told him how much or how little it was safe or convenient to make public.

"Starting to feel like summer," Larson said. And he squinted out where the morning light was still glancing unpredictably off the water.

Phil, too, looked out at the yachts and beyond them, across to Rangitoto. "Nice weather for sailing," he said, and they both laughed.

"What can I do for you Phil," Larson asked.

Phil went straight to the point. "I know about your surveillance at Harry Butler's place. Don't worry. He hasn't been indiscreet. He's an old friend, and he knows this is one of the subjects I deal with on the paper. When you have the drug squad sitting in your house it's not a bad idea to look for advice."

"You know he booted us out," Larson said.

"Do you blame him? You were lucky he let you in."

"We needed more time. You know how it is. Jump too soon and you can waste a year's patient work."

"But you can't expect . . ."

"I don't expect anything, pal. I just go on being hopeful." And Larson lit a cigarette.

"Put yourself in his position," Phil said. "He's got a family to protect."

"His family wasn't in danger. You know how these characters work. They're dangerous to one another. If they think they're being watched they just bugger off."

"I think you got a pretty good deal out of Harry. How long were you in his house?"

"Look, pal, you don't have to defend the prof. He doesn't owe us anything. When he'd had enough we said thanks and packed it in. What does he want now? A certificate?"

Phil's expression remained neutral. After a moment he said, "And you didn't get any further with Greg Carey."

"We moved it along a bit. We know he's dealing. The money's rolling in – we've been able to verify that. But we don't know where he's getting his stuff. Not yet – not for sure."

"There's someone bigger . . ."

"There's always someone bigger these days. The Greg Careys used to run their own operations, but not any more. There's the big supplier. And a lawyer to launder the money."

"The usual one?"

"The usual three."

"Macready?"

Larson nodded. "He's been down there once or twice."

Phil hesitated. He seemed to want to frame the next question carefully. "Does Macready own a piece of land anywhere? I mean a bit of coastline?"

Larson smiled. "If he does he hasn't told us. And it's not likely to be registered in his name. Why? Have you got something to tell us?"

Phil shook his head. "Not yet."

There was another silence while they stared out across the harbour entrance. Without looking at Phil, speaking quietly, Larson said, "It would be nice if you two would tell me what you know."

Phil looked at him. "What two?"

"You and your old school-mate Harry. I'd like to know, just for starters, who tipped off Greg Carey and his girl that we were watching."

"Were they tipped off?"

"The girl used to spend half her life in front of a mirror. Posing. Dancing. You could see it from the Butler's kitchen. Then one day she just stopped. And a day or so later when we went through the house with a dog there was nothing."

"Maybe he wasn't dealing from the house."

"So all those callers John here got pictures of were just friends and relations."

Phil considered it. "O.K. So he was dealing from the house. And then someone warned him he was being watched. Why didn't he just – as you said before – bugger off?"

"Better to be searched first and have us find nothing isn't it? Put us off the scent."

"So who would have warned them?"

"Like to know?" Larson Snow looked like a man who'd

decided to fly a kite. "I think it might have been your old mate, the prof."

Phil laughed. "You've been watching too many movies."

"You think you know him well enough to be sure?"

"Of course. And even if I didn't – why would he let you into his house to watch, and then tip them off about it? It doesn't make sense."

"You haven't done surveillance work. People change when you watch them every day. I mean they don't change but you do. You start to like them. They have their human side, you see. You start to think do I want to put him, or her – especially her – away for eight or ten or twelve years. It gets at you as the days go by. You're not telling me Harry Butler hasn't got a human heart are you?"

"No I'm not. But if that happened he'd tell you to pack your gear and leave."

"Well he did didn't he?"

"Yes but you say they were warned earlier. The girl stopped posing in front of the mirror."

"Just like that. A dead stop. One day she's back and forth to the mirror like a bloody yo-yo. Next day she never goes near it. And curtains go across the bedroom at night. That hadn't happened before."

Phil shook his head. He rejected the idea, but he said nothing.

"I've got a theory," Larson said, "and I'm going to tell you what it is. I don't think I want your mate to know about it just yet but I'm not going to ask you to swear you won't tell him because I think you'd probably refuse. And anyway I don't know what a promise like that would be worth. So I'll just say I'd rather you didn't tell him. Take it as something strictly off the record."

"It's up to you what you tell me," Phil said.

"I spent a lot of time in that Butler house," Larson said. "You wander round. You get the feel of things. You have to fill in a lot of time when nothing's happening and maybe nobody's home. I got to looking at their photo albums. Mrs Butler didn't seem to mind if I took things off their book-shelves. She's a nice lady, Mrs Butler . . ."

Phil agreed. "Very nice. I'm very fond of her."

"The prof seems to do a lot of travelling."

"He gets leave. And gets invited to conferences."

"He takes his camera. It looked as though Mrs Butler had sorted all the photographs into those albums. She's written a note under each photograph. Now . . ."

Larson took out his cigarettes again. "Sure you won't smoke?"

Phil shook his head. Larson lit up and thought for a moment, drawing in the smoke.

"We've known about Greg Carey for quite a long time. We lost track of him. In fact we thought he was dead. Then he turned up in Auckland with this Mandy Rivers. She's new to us, but the Aussies had stuff on her. Back at Central the boys have spent a lot of time filling in her past. She's like your pal Harry. Does a lot of travelling. Mostly to Australia, but she's made trips to interesting places like Thailand and Indonesia and Hong Kong and Singapore."

"Makes sense," Phil said.

"It fits the picture doesn't it. The Greg Careys push the risks off on to their women. In those small operations it was mostly the girls who came through Customs with the stuff. If they got caught their boyfriends disappeared. Didn't want to know about it. So we figure before Carey got into a big syndicate Mandy Rivers was travelling for him. She doesn't seem to have had a funny passport.

Central was able to put together a list of her trips. There was one a couple of years back – to Singapore. You with me?"

Phil said he was.

"This is where luck comes into it. I mean if what you trip over turns out to be useful, it's luck. If it's not useful it's just confusing. What happened was I was looking at one of those albums of the Butlers just a day after I got the list of Mandy Rivers" travels and there were some shots of Singapore. He was there on his own. You can pick the trips he made solo because when he travels with his wife they photograph one another. Mrs Butler's notes in the albums always give dates. You see where I'm heading?"

Phil was frowning. "I think I do. It doesn't amount to very much."

"Well it might amount to a lot or a little. But the fact is Mandy Rivers and your mate Butler were in Singapore on the same dates a couple of years ago."

"Along with a million others."

"Right. Probably nearer two million. I haven't forgotten the others. But they were there. They didn't arrive together, and I don't know whether they left on the same day, but it must have been close. And they stayed at the same hotel."

Phil said, "I don't have to tell you Harry Butler wouldn't have anything to do with smuggling drugs. And if you thought he did you wouldn't be telling me this."

"Right." Larson nodded.

"So what's the point?"

"Let me tell you one other thing. There was a photograph missing from the Singapore trip. You could see the space where it had been in the album, and there was one of Mrs Butler's notes under it."

"I suppose it said 'Harry's friend Mandy'."

"It said something like 'Street in Singapore'. But just think about it. If you met a nice little girl in Singapore and you wanted to keep a photograph of her but you didn't want anyone to know about it, what would you do?"

Phil shook his head. "I never have these problems. What would you do?"

"What about a photo of a city street. Lots of people about and you don't know any of them. Mostly locals – Chinese and Indians – but some tourists as well. But right there near the camera is the girl you want to keep a picture of. She just looks like part of the crowd."

Phil shook his head again. "You have a dirty mind."

"And your pal has a reputation."

"I know about the reputation," Phil said. "I think around the university you only have to look alive and well to have a reputation."

"But just suppose that's how it happened. When would you take the pic out of the album? It's like a riddle. Question: when would you take it out? Answer: when the girl turned up as your next-door neighbour."

"I will have a cigarette after all," Phil said. When he'd lit it he said, "If it had been like that Harry wouldn't have let you in."

"Wrong. He'd let us in because at first he'd be scared. He'd want to show us he was clean. Then when he'd had time to think about it he'd start to worry. Would he want to help us put away a girl he'd had a nice time with? Sooner or later he'd warn her. Finally, when we'd been there long enough he'd pretend his nerve had cracked. Throw a wobbly. Boot us out. I thought a lot about that after it happened. Right out of the blue. Young Jack here has his camera trained on someone getting out of a car in

92

the drive and all of a sudden the prof. goes off like a rocket. 'Out of my house. I've had enough. You're disrupting my life.' That kind of thing. But he's not the kind of guy who blows his stack. It's not his style. He was putting it on – I'm fucking sure of it."

"Because of Mandy Rivers?"

"Because of Mandy Rivers, pal. Precisely."

"It's a nice theory. Why did you tell me?"

"I'm not sure. I think maybe I thought you might be able to talk me out of it."

"I don't think you're right."

Larson smiled and shook his head. "You'd have to do better than that."

"So you really believe it."

"I think it's likely. It's probably not important. I mean if your mate had some fun with this Mandy in Singapore and he wants to hide it, that's fine. That's his business. But if he's put her up to the fact that we're on her boyfriend's tail, he's a bloody nuisance."

Phil threw the cigarette away unfinished. He said nothing.

"I'm still not sure why you suggested we meet," Larson said.

"Well . . ." Phil looked as if he wasn't sure himself. "You know this is one of my subjects on the paper. And when Harry told me you'd been using his house I felt protective. I know more about what you're dealing with than he does. I wanted to get into the picture."

"Well you're in it now," Larson said. "How do you feel about it?"

"Fantasyland," Phil said. But he said it good-humouredly.

They were walking towards their cars. "Keep in

touch," Larson said. "And don't write anything that will get in our way. I want to put Greg Carey inside if I can, but he's only the little bugger. I've got my harpoon sharpened up for something bigger, if I can only get the right chance."

"Good luck," Phil said. "Don't let your imagination run away with your harpoon."

FIFTEEN

A Sunday in Milan

The day is so quiet it must be Sunday. I walk out into the Corso Magenta and there are a few parked cars but no one in sight. Not even any activity around the church of Santa Maria. The tram tracks stretch away and they seem to emphasize the silence. It's cold but the sun has come out. It strikes across the street, lighting up the concrete balconies on which no one appears. The road looks a dark colour – something like navy blue, shading into black. Up at the intersection there's some movement – a yellow Alfa Romeo, a dark blue Fiat, an orange bus, a man in an overcoat and gloves with a cloth cap, moving purposefully. I'm glad of these signs of life. The sun picks out the texture in the castle wall – its arrow holes and crenellations. There's something tactile about the way the brickwork on the curved tower is defined in light and shade. The trees in front of it have lost their last leaves.

Around a block. Yes, it's Sunday, and the city is beginning to stir. My head aches. Too much wine last night, and no sign of Uta all day. I ought to be glad of a rest from her, but I miss her when she doesn't appear. I keep stopping to look through iron grilles and gateways, under stone and plaster arches, at enclosed gardens, ornamental pools, fountains and tubbed trees. Every entrance reminds me in some small or large detail of the Consulate. I've only been there once by invitation, but sometimes I make that

95

the direction of my afternoon walk. Then I go past without stopping, afraid of the embarrassment of being seen to have come uninvited.

The sun is holding its own, there's more and more light pouring into the nooks and crannies of Milan, but no warmth in it. The air is sharp, unusually clear, and bitterly cold. Over my shoulder I carry the leather bag in which there are essentials like my passport, my chequebook, my credit cards, my current reading. There is also the blue folder. It feels heavy today, a dead weight, and silent.

Something is happening in front of the railway station – some public works involving huge yellow cranes and metal hoppers. The station itself, blind and deaf, looks as though it's remembering Mussolini – but with difficulty. An orange tram goes by, its metal rod against the overhead wire raised as in the fascist salute.

I thought today because it's Sunday and because of the effects of last night's wine I wouldn't work. And I would stay away from the café. But why in that case is the blue folder in my bag? It isn't long before I'm back at the Corso Magenta. I hesitate at the gate of the Palazzo delle Stelline but I walk on and turn in to the café. I haven't been expecting to see Uta but she's there in her usual place. She and the padrone greet me warmly. They've been wondering why I'm not at work already. As Uta touches my hand I feel the weight of my bag lighten. It's almost as if the blue folder has moved a little, like a child moving in the womb.

I'm embarrassed by this fantasy of course, as I am by most of the random thoughts that make their way through my head on a morning after drinking. But now my two friends are talking to me about the scene at the shark aquarium. The padrone likes it. Uta is indifferent – it's not a scene she cares about greatly, one way or the other. But she has a question ("an important question" she calls it) for me. Was Harry really in Singapore with Mandy Rivers?

I have to find a way of telling her that the Story makes decisions about when and in what order details like that will be released. But I admit that it doesn't seem unreasonable, on the basis of what has already been revealed, to assume that he was. At least it seems clear that he was there at the same time. And that could explain how it is he knows her. In other words it seems to me Larson Snow was engaging in some pretty intelligent guesswork.

Yes yes yes, says the padrone – si si si. He's excited and speaks rapidly in Italian, but Uta, whose Italian is as good as her English, translates for me. Yes, he agrees, good guessing by Larson Snow; but he got something wrong didn't he? He thought Harry had asked the drug squad to leave because of Mandy. Larson picked that Harry's tantrum was trumped up; but it never occurred to him that it had anything to do with the particular person whose face was about to be photographed.

I agree with the padrone. So Jason was for the moment protected.

But that was what Uta wanted to know – protected from what? Jason had met them at the Turf Bar and said he was in the money. He must have said more than that, but how he came to be in the money hadn't yet been revealed. When Phil talked to Larson Snow he must have known already where the money was coming from. But of course he didn't mention Jason. He couldn't. And what Phil must have learned from that conversation by the shark aquarium was that the drug squad had no notion of Jason's existence.

I agree. And I add that that was probably Phil's real

reason for the meeting. He wanted to know whether Larson Snow had any idea of why Harry had evicted them. What emerged was that Larson had half an idea and it was half right. But Jason Cook didn't figure in his calculations.

But I tell them I think the best way to move nearer to answers to all these questions is to take them back to a particular morning in Auckland. The morning of the rain storm. That way, I hope, the whole picture will begin to become clearer.

SIXTEEN

A Saturday in Auckland

Saturday morning, early December. The air hot, heavy, humid and still, the sky darkening, until it breaks with a single crack like a starting pistol. The rain comes down very precisely, the clear crystal drops bouncing on the warm roadway as if they were hailstones. Then a rumbling in the wings, heavy cannon, explosions. The drops get bigger, then very big. The air seems filled with water. Or as if, through the water, float pockets of air.

Mass on mass, the clouds and the explosions pile up on one another. The rustle of water everywhere running, like crowds gathering or scattering, gets louder, less rustle than rush; and overlaying it, finally rendering it indistinguishable (though still it's there) the drumming on the iron roofs becomes a continuous roar. Only the thunderclaps speak above it.

The sky is a heavy grey striped with black, like that shirt of Harry Butler's emerging in the white porcelain dish in John Sprott's darkroom. Through the sky's stripes, cutting across them, cracking the tight dark bowl held down over the Auckland isthmus, the white fractures of lightning open and heal, open again and again heal.

Still the raindrops get larger. They pelt and break like flowers over the window glass. Snow-flake size, but falling fast, crashing, no life in them after impact. They might be the bodies of small animals, frogs or goldfish or sparrows, hurled out of the heavens, rejects. But nothing piles up on lawns or in garden beds. Everything is liquid, everything turning downhill, looking for a way out, crowding the exits, rushing down slopes, panicking to find the sea. Water becomes more water becomes more-water. Its urgency can't be ignored. One of the Four Elements is in revolt. Make room for it or it will make room for itself. Drains are blocking. Brooms are out. Voices are shouting through and between the drumming and the explosions. Laughing too. O what a lovely war! Children are out in it, whooping, sodden. This revolution permits the carmagnole but not the guillotine.

John Sprott pauses in his work to listen, then carries on. He can't stop now. He's re-doing the four or five shots he fired off that last morning in the Butlers' kitchen, all of them obstructed by Harry Butler's rain-sky shirt-front. He's blowing them up and there's one in which he finds half a face, or maybe a little more than half, distinguishable. He's watching it form in the dish, trying to ignore the racket outside, but it's not willing to ignore him. "John." The voice is urgent on the other side of the dark-room door. "John. Quick. It's coming into the kitchen."

In Mt Albert, standing on his front verandah watching it sweeping past the eucalypts on the hilltop and down into the valley suburb, Larson Snow tries and fails to keep his mind on some inner calculus that will tell him what it was he missed in his conversation yesterday with Phil Gardner. He can feel the air cooling as the rain gets heavier. It clears his head. Now there's lightning around that crown of eucalypts, and playing along the tops of the Waitakeres, bringing them momentarily into view through their cloud-shroud. He tries to go over it once more. The drumming on his roof gets louder. The guttering along the verandah front won't take the volume of water, which spills out and spreads over the lawn. He watches rings forming and intersecting and destroying one another on the broadening surface of the lawn-lake. How can you think in this engulfing white-out of sound? But why should you want to? As of now, Larson tells himself, he couldn't give a fuck if the whole world was going to disappear up its own nostril in one gigantic snort.

Across town in Ponsonby Phil and Kiri Gardner are trapped in the supermarket with a trolley full of food, watching the weather do for Phil the carwash he keeps putting off from one weekend to the next. In the carpark all the metal colours come up distinct as they lose their hard edges in the blur of the downpour, while on the asphalt under them a million drops in a moment join hands to make a black lake, putting themselves into some *Guinness Book of Records* that will be remaindered before lunch. Phil's laugh in Ponsonby echoes Larson's in Mt Albert. Who cares what Macready may be importing, or how? Is it stored somewhere safe? Can he keep his powder dry?

Harry Butler is swimming at Mission Bay. The water has been oily smooth, swelling and declining as if the body of the sea were breathing, but the surface unbroken under the heavy-humid sky. Now the storm breaks over it, no wind, just the fireworks overhead, and then the downpour. Great drops dimple the smooth surface and are gone, their life's ambition achieved in an instant. Not for them the landward struggle, over and through and around and between. Integration. Union. Consummation. The Many becoming the One.

Harry, a long way out, rides up and down with the sea's breathing, his body relishing its weightlessness, his skin recovering its own life in the perfect water, the muscles of his arms and legs and back seeming to make their own accommodations with the moving element as if they were native to it, his head (that philosophical head, Head of Department, head of a household, the Head-that-Claire-Caressed like the House-that-Jack-Built) held clear, listening and looking, tasting salt, enjoying the rain's dousing, catching the waft of shellfish and seaweed that drifts from the reef.

The drops grow larger, more concentrated. Images blur into one another, the storm wiping the slate clean of everything but itself – water, with its assistant electricity, showing what it can do with a world that relies on it for reasonable and controlled behaviour.

At number 27 Arvon Crescent Mandy Rivers is out on the balcony, her favourite stereo tape defeated by the drumming on iron that comes up from the streets below. Down on the lawn the little boys next door who are the sons of Harry Butler are capering in the flood that has come up out of the stormwater drain under number 25, crosses the drive of 27, and disappears under the Butler house. Now Greg's sports turns into the drive, swishes through the flood and into the carport from which Greg, his leather jacket pulled up around his head, emerges bent double and running. There's the moment it takes him to get up the stairs and out on to the balcony and now he's there beside her. She's slow to register that his mood and hers are not the same. He's not capering and dancing with pleasure. He's shouting and pointing up, angry because she doesn't at once understand and respond. He lunges at her in a kind of side-swipe that pushes her aside as he pulls himself up into the kiwi fruit vine and climbs quickly through the falling sky.

And "O look Mum," and "Hey Mum LOOK" Jonah

and Reuben shout from their river boat on the lawn. "Greg Carey's climbing on to the roof." And Claire Butler watching from the kitchen and worrying what happens to the water that's gathering under their house thinks "That's something I'd rather we hadn't seen."

How can one weather affect so many people in such different ways? In Mt Eden Louise Lamont has been trying to be civil to a research student whose name might be Matthew or Mark or Luke or John. Once he might have seemed desirable. Once he probably did seem desirable – faintly she recalls that he did. Then his name would have been distinctly present to her. Then she would have taken more care, and been more volubly grateful, arranging in a vase the three tiger lilies he has brought her. She might even have found the way he lounges on her couch sexy and inviting, and responded more positively than with an only half-good-humoured shrugging away, to the touch of his hand at the back of her neck. Her indifference has made her angry, much angrier with herself than with Matthew Mark Luke or John; and much angrier with Harry Butler than with herself. Because her indifference is Harry's fault; and what makes it worse is that she has begun to believe Harry doesn't want her, that he would like to be relieved (even at the same time that he wouldn't like it at all) of the painful pressure Louise knows she has become in his life. She knows it but she can't help it and she doesn't want to be reminded of it.

The research student is young and handsome and eligible and attentive – all the things Harry is not – and Louise looks at him and consults herself inwardly trying to discover some stir of interest. Finding none she feels irritable. She wants to be rid of him and has almost got him to the door when the gods open their vaults in the sky and tell

103

her with a bolt of lightning and a bucket of rain that they won't make it easy for her. Matthew is not to be sent out into this prodigious and (to him) heaven-sent downpour. He must be allowed back to sprawl again, to touch (this time she doesn't shrug away) the back of her neck, to caress, to kiss, and finally (will it be?) to persuade her into her own bedroom full of photographs, and presents, reminders of Harry Butler. On the unmade bed, among books half-read and letters half-written, the head of Louise Lamont thinks of Harry so that her body can begin to enjoy itself.

North of Auckland the storm can be seen and heard from a distance. The gunfire sounds from far off and the flashes light the sky. There's less turbulence – simply rain, heavy and continuous. It forces Jason Cook, cutting a track through manuka, sweating inside his oilskin, to give up. He lays his tools aside in the mud beside the path, along with the wood and steel rods and bags of loose metal he's using to make steps where the going gets steep. Spade, grubber, axe and hammers – he puts them in a neat line, beside the pile of pine stakes, covers them with a plastic sheet and puts stones at the corners. Then he makes his way up through the bush, skirting the stream, looking down from the ridge into deep pools and seeing them turn brown as the volume of water increases. At the top of the ridge he comes to a small clearing in front of his hut. He goes up on to the verandah, takes off his oilskin and shakes it out. Inside, he dries his hands and lights a cigarette, then returns to the verandah to stand smoking, looking down over the bush to the little bay and the anchorage, the jetty off which he fishes in the evenings, and a single yacht anchored offshore. The rain drums on the iron roof of the verandah and Jason relaxes, drawing in the smoke, thinking of the money he's stacking away – the best he has made in years, and in cash worth half as much again because he has no intention of declaring it to the Department of Internal Revenue. Money from heaven, like this rain, sudden and unexpected. Take it while it's offering. It won't last.

A single tui lands on a flax stalk, perches at an angle on the angled stalk, its glossy black head bobbing nervously, its white tuft laundered. Jason stands quite still. The bird works quickly up the stalk, poking its beak into each flower. At the top of the stalk there's a pause, but no song. In a flash of black and a whir of wings it's away towards the next ridge.

The rain is getting heavier. It's forming a channel down the edge of the cleared patch. Something shines there. Jason notices it, then forgets, his eye following the line the tui has taken. Down in the bay the water seems to swell very gently under the drumming of the rain. The yacht turns a little, rides, settles. There's no one down there. There never is. This bay is surrounded by private land. Even the owner of the yacht is unknown to Jason.

He flicks his butt away over the verandah rail. His eye returns to the flax flowers, then to the brown channel the rain is making, and to that shiny something he sees now as a half-moon, uncovered by the loosened soil. He pulls on his oilskin and goes down to it. He digs with his hands in the soft wet earth, pulling away grass-roots and sticks and piles of leaves, then scraping at the covering of soil. He can see now it's the top of a drum, like an oil drum, sealed. He stops, and looks away into the falling rain. There's a strange calm takes hold of him in this kind of weather. Does he really want to know what's inside a drum someone has taken the trouble to bury? Curiosity killed the cat and at this moment this cat is strangely lacking in curiosity. He allows himself to fall backward against the base of the flax bush. From this place he can see nothing but reedy grasses and the rain-black peeling trunks of manuka. The rain beats on his oilskin hood.

At Mission Bay now Harry Butler has come ashore. He's drying himself in the empty changing shed, rubbing his body slowly with a rough red towel. Outside, the rain still falls, but without thunder the sound seems a kind of loud silence.

Sensation. Body. Himself, inside the cocoon of silent sound. The problems which nag at him and which it's his professional duty to unravel and tease out, weave themselves together into a pattern. For a moment the image of Wittgenstein comes to him, not with the usual sense of awe and respect, but with pity. A poor bodiless brilliant head – a head on a platter, thinking. That could be himself too, a smaller Wittgenstein not on a platter but on a saucer in the kitchen of philosophy, except that thank Christ it's not himself, because his body has rebelled against that unravelling which reveals not a pattern but a tangle of threads.

In Mt Roskill John Sprott has stemmed the small flood in the kitchen and he's back in his darkroom where the half face has formed itself in the dish. It's not a face he knows, but he will take it to his boss on Monday.

And in Mt Albert his boss hasn't moved from the verandah. The lawn lake is static now, and he's thinking "Macready". That was Phil Gardner's question – the one he ought to have stuck to: Might Macready have a piece of land somewhere on the coast? Of course he might; and maybe the newsman who likes to play detective knows where it is.

In Ponsonby the newsman and his wife Kiri have made a

106

dash for it to their washed car. The trolleyful of shopping has been unloaded on to the back seat and Phil is trying to clear a fog off the inside of the windscreen.

At number 27 Arvon Crescent Greg Carey is anxiously checking his little polythene bags, weighed and ready for the street, brought down from the roof where they're kept in plastic lunch boxes with tight seals, held in place by a brick among the branches of the vine. It's all perfectly dry and he's worrying now that he went up the vine in broad daylight and was probably seen by those brats still boating on the lawn next door. In the kitchen Mandy is making baked beans on toast for lunch, with a poached egg to go on top. It will be her first real meal for twenty-four hours. All of a sudden the rain has made her hungry.

And in number 29, Claire, who's trying to become Sophia, is on the phone, not to the City Council to send a pumping truck because the flood from number 25 has crossed the lawn of 27 and formed a lake under her house, but to Duag MacPherson. He's telling her he understands her problem but she must try harder to stay focused – to keep her eyes on the symbol and let it absorb her thoughts. "It will draw your thinking out of your head," he tells her. "Just stay focused on the symbol."

She has it in front of her while she listens to his hypnotic and really rather hateful voice (in some moods she likes Harry's description of him as the carpet seller). The symbol is a perfect circle formed by two interlocking shapes that look like dolphins, one black, one white. The white dolphin has a black eye, the black one a white eye. She thinks they may be copulating. She thinks too that that's not what she's supposed to think, or to see. "Remember that everything depends on your focus," the voice tells her. "Stay focused on the symbol."

107

In bed in Mt Eden Louise Lamont props her head on the pillows and watches Matthew walking naked about her bedroom, looking at her books and pictures and her pieces of pottery and glass. She doesn't like him looking at her things but she remains silent. So does he. He was silent all the time they were making love, and then he was out of bed, restless, still silent. He has a beautiful body. She admires his shoulders, and his buttocks, and his strong legs, as he stands with his back to her, flicking through a book of photographs of Picasso. The rain is falling steadily now, heavy, but no longer violent. Has he been struck dumb in the act of love? Even at the end there wasn't much more than a grunt, or a clearing of the throat. It's like being made love to by a machine, she thinks. But now here I am with the machine in my bedroom. What am I supposed to do with it?

She thinks of Harry and feels remorse, though why she should feel anything at all except satisfaction is mysterious to her. I'm supposed to be trained in logic, she thinks. Harry Butler trains you in logic in the classroom, then he trains you out of it on the floor. She feels a tightening in the throat. That's tears, she thinks. Here they come. And she tries to turn her mind again to the restless apostle Matthew, fiddling with her things . . .

Could we make it (let's allow for a moment an impossible intersection of times as well as places) that one of those things his hand lights on is a postcard of the *Last Supper* painted by Leonardo on a wall of an annexe to the Church of Santa Maria delle Grazie in the Corso Magenta, Milan?

In the Palazzo delle Stelline I wake from these dreams of Auckland. I go out into the dark of the balcony. Snow is falling. It's covering the orange tiled roofs and drifting down into the courtyard. It's flurrying and eddying around the octagon top and pinnacle of Santa Maria. Uta Haverstrom has escaped the snow. She and the Consul have driven south to Rapallo where they have an old farmhouse among olive groves above the town. A feeling of loneliness invades me and I return to bed and try to summon back the dream of Auckland, the storm, the thunder, the flood, and Louise watching from her bed while Matthew looks at the postcard of the *Last Supper*. But what comes to me as I close my eyes and drift towards sleep again is not Louise Lamont. It's Jason Cook. I see the half-face that's to go from John Sprott's dish into Larson Snow's in-tray, still leaning back against the flax bush in the rain, his hand playing idly with loose soil around the exposed half-moon of the buried drum. His eyes are turned towards the next ridge from which comes, as from half a world away, the notes of a tui, indescribably beautiful.

SEVENTEEN

Leaving Milan

That snow, and Uta's departure south – I'd thought they might bring me luck. I'd started to think of Uta as a burden, but I was wrong. Now I was stuck. The voice in my head, which I thought of as the voice from the blue folder, was silent. The Story was missing its quarrels with Uta and didn't feel quite safe without them.

I tried to be systematic, orderly. In the past when I'd run into problems I'd taken long brisk walks about the city. But in the district around the Corso Magenta the snow hadn't been swept. I suppose they expected it to melt but it didn't and now it was frozen. You picked your way along, sliding and saving yourself. The local hospital had run out of plaster of Paris, there had been so many broken bones. The best I could do out of doors was make my way down to the café.

The padrone welcomed me as usual and left me pretty much alone. Now we didn't have Uta to translate the difficult bits, our conversation had gone back to basics. He left me to work, encouraging me now and then from behind the machine with phrases like "Let 'em have it, Maestro" picked up from American movies on late night television. Sometimes, if business wasn't brisk and a loud conversation started up near me, he would find another table for the talkers, pretending it would be more comfortable for them, or warmer, but really moving them away so I wouldn't be disturbed.

I made marks on paper. I stared thoughtfully at the ceiling for his benefit. But nothing was happening. I tried working in my room. I even, guiltily, tried another café. None of these things helped. I was hopelessly stuck.

Notes began to come up from Rapallo. Then phone calls. Uta wanted me to say what had happened when Harry and Mandy were in Singapore. I consulted the Story. It had no objections. It made no reply. I told Uta that was as good a place as any to go next, but still nothing went down on paper.

Uta was very particular in her questioning. I wanted to conceal from her that I was stuck. It seemed unprofessional – something to be ashamed of. But it was no use trying to hide it from her. She knew. "How many pages today," she asked, and I had to tell her "None."

"Think it out loud," she told me. "Tell me what you want to put down next. You've done that before. It helps you get started."

I tried, but my mind went blank. I felt as if I was losing my grip on the facts. She had phoned me at the café and the padrone was standing behind me holding his hands together over his stomach in a pose that suggested anxiety.

"Listen," Uta said. "Didn't Harry tell Phil about what happened in Singapore?"

"Yes," I replied. "Of course he did. Phil pestered him and in the end he spilled the beans."

"Well there you have it," she said. "Put down that conversation between Harry and Phil."

I thanked her. I pretended it was just the advice I needed. But of course I knew perfectly well that was where I had to go next. The problem was that nothing came of it when I tried. It's difficult to explain. All I can

111

say is it seemed as if the voice from the blue folder had fallen silent.

Two days later I phoned Uta. I admitted I was no further on. "Do you think it's the snow," I asked. "Maybe stories hibernate. Like bears."

She assured me it wasn't so. "We in the north know about such things," she said. "In winter stories come to life. Haven't you heard of *A Winter's Tale*?"

Because of her accent it came through to me as something like *Arvinter's Tale*, and for a moment I had to ask who Arvinter was.

"You know," she said. "*A Winter's Tale*. By Shakespeare."

This little misunderstanding was of no consequence except that it caused me to recognize the affection I felt for this woman the voice from the blue folder liked to call ironically the Great Dane.

"I'll try again," I told her; and I rather hoped she would pick up the note of hopelessness in my voice. In fact I was wishing she would come back to Milan.

Half an hour later the phone rang again. Now she had a suggestion. She thought I should come and work in Rapallo. Erik had had to return to the Milan Consulate and he'd taken with him the number one car. Uta needed wheels, especially living in a cottage in the hills overlooking the town. She'd spoken to Erik on the phone and he was quite willing for me to take the number two car down to her. She would find a cheap hotel and book a room for me.

All this had an immediate effect. It was as if already I could hear the voice from the blue folder. I didn't hesitate. I thanked her profusely and told her to expect me.

I was sorry to be saying goodbye to the Palace of the Little Stars, and my split-level room, and my balcony with its view of Santa Maria delle Grazie. But I didn't have any doubt that I had to go. The Story, it seemed, had grown to depend on Uta's Nordic jostling and bullying. Maybe it wasn't even indifferent to those sweaters of hers which had lately been figuring prominently in my snow-bound dreams.

I paid my bill and carried my suitcase down to the café, slipping and sliding on the frozen snow. The padrone was sorry I was leaving but he was pleased I would be joining Uta. When I was a famous writer, he told me, people would come to his café and ask about me. Like Hemingway's café in Paris (he'd seen it on television) – La Closerie des Lilas where *The Sun Also Rises* was written.

"I tell you work today get drunk to the night," he said. "I tell you good guy."

He held on to my handshake, banging my upper arm with his free hand. "In spring you come back," he said. "Write more."

I nodded and smiled although I didn't believe it. He called a taxi to take me to the Consulate. There the number two car was waiting for me, and so was the Consul.

Erik Haverstrom was courteous, formal, helpful with advice and warnings about my drive. He gave me a pile of books for Uta, and some extra clothes. "Even down there it can be cold," he told me.

My drive out of Milan was not uneventful but it's unimportant. I slid on the ice and got stuck on the tramtracks. I took wrong turnings. I was given wrong directions. Horns blared at me (all my fault – Scusi) and I was given the fingers more than once. Probably the evil eye as well. That hideous autostrada south seemed like a haven when I reached it. The open road! And on the seat beside me the blue folder!

113

Ahead lay the Mediterranean – terraced hillslopes and smoky-grey olives. I could see them in my mind long before I reached Genoa. I wondered why it should have taken Uta to persuade me that was where I ought to go.

As I left the outskirts of Genoa and headed east along the coast road I imagined I could hear the Story beside me. It wasn't talking. It was singing under its breath (the final deep note only barely audible above the purr of the number two car's engine) Baron Ocks's song from *Der Rosenkavalier*.

EIGHTEEN

Bernard Shaw and the Actress

When Harry Butler told Phil Gardner about his Singapore adventure they were in an inflatable rubber dinghy off Mission Bay. Harry had had the boys out in the boat. He'd had Claire out in it too, and she'd swum ashore. Now she and Kiri had taken the boys back to the house, and Phil and Harry paddled out, idly stopping to lie back in the sun, drifting and looking at the waterfront from the sea. It was in fact the day after the rainstorm – a Sunday, and the sky and the sea and the suburbs looked like those cars in the carpark of the Ponsonby supermarket – washed clean, bright, glittering. The storm had gone as quickly as it came. There was no evidence it had been, except that uncanny brightness with which every edge cut and every surface threw back the light – and perhaps also a residual heaviness in the feel of the air on your skin.

Harry recounted it in a random, dreamy non-sequence, like the drifting of their boat. Occasionally he got interested in his own story, and sat up. Then he lapsed back again. Phil was alert. He asked questions. He tried hard to see it (he'd never been to Singapore) and to understand it. He took trouble over it, as if it had been a news story. So you could say in the end Phil's head contained a more exact record of those two or three days than Harry's did. The facts came from Harry, but it was Phil who put them together, and Phil who drew the conclusion.

So we begin with Harry Butler arriving at Singapore Airport and taking the coach to his hotel. He was on his way back from a conference in Delhi and he'd decided to be a tourist for a couple of days. It was evening, and getting out of the air-conditioned coach he was hit by the heat and humidity – and by his first impressions of those tree-lined streets with broad pavements, and the crowd of oriental faces that looked so uniformly young and beautiful.

Between the coach-stop and the hotel's main door he was offered a woman, a girl, a boy, some drugs. An Indian in a turban seemed to take pity on him. "This man is suffering from jet-lag. Leave him alone. Make way there." And having driven off the touts with a swagger stick the Indian helped him with his bag. "You're tired, sir. You like me to send nice girl to your room. She give you good fuck."

Inside the foyer – a huge area, with palms and vines growing out of pots, and fountains and pools and marble statues, like an indoor park – Harry saw among the crowd the girl he would later know as Mandy. She was standing awkwardly, watching the new arrivals. She looked at the labels on his bag and said "Oh New Zealand", and smiled. He smiled back, and forgot all about her until he saw her again next morning.

Scene Two has Harry at breakfast. Mandy appears, looks around the room, and sits at Harry's table. He looks up to say good morning and recognizes her as the girl who noticed his New Zealand labels the night before. But having chosen to sit with him, she avoids his eye. When he addresses a remark to her she answers only briefly, as if protecting herself from strangers. She seems to Harry odd – and then once again he forgets about her.

116

Next we see him in one of those arcades above the street, with many small shops. An Indian is running after him offering to make him a suit overnight at a very cheap price. But Harry's not interested in clothes for himself. He's looking for something for Claire – maybe some shirts, or a dress if he can find something in her size that he feels confident she will like. And he wants some toys for Jonah and Reuben.

We should see him in a number of places – shopping arcades, out on those broad sidewalks under the trees, in the botanical gardens, in the post office, back in the hotel lobby. I'm not sure how much time went by before he saw Mandy again, but I think it was the same day. This time she came up beside him and tugged at his arm and told him in that baby voice that reminded him of Marilyn Monroe that she'd had breakfast with him at the hotel and here they were running into one another again, wasn't it surprising?

It didn't seem surprising to Harry but he was glad to talk to her. They were both finding the heat almost unbearable so they went back to the hotel and had something – possibly it was lunch – in the air-conditioned restaurant. Later they went to a movie, and to a bar, and back to the shopping arcades. Mandy helped him choose something for Claire. They seemed to get to know one another quickly. Mandy still seemed odd to Harry, but there was something charming about her. He felt a distinct quickening of interest, which she appeared to encourage. She touched him often. She patted his arm, or squeezed it when she was pleased, or punched it when he made a joke. She tossed her hair against his face and pressed against him in lifts. Now and then she broke into a few lines of a popular song, singing them to him and bobbing about under his nose. As Harry told it to Phil, all the signals

117

seemed quite unambiguous. Put crudely the question was not would she but should they – and Harry thought Why should they not? He was in a strange land. He wouldn't see her again. They would enjoy it and it would do no harm to anyone ... And so on. The familiar arguments are recorded only to register how ordinary the situation was. Or seemed.

That evening they danced at the hotel. Mandy's hair was pressed against his face. Her pelvis was pushed against his. Why should he have expected any conclusion different from the one he did expect? But when he took her to her room and went to kiss her, she pretended to be surprised. Is it possible she was surprised? Harry couldn't believe it. But she became once again the girl at the breakfast table, who had sat with him and then avoided his eye, as if she were Little Red Riding Hood saving herself from the Wolf in the forest of a Singapore hotel.

Harry felt a small surge of anger. Or irritation. Not because she didn't want him in her bed, but because her behaviour seemed quite clearly to have invited what she now rejected. He shrugged, shook his head, patted her and told her she was a puzzle. Then he said goodnight and set off down the corridor towards the lifts. She ran after him, tugging at his sleeve. "Now I've hurt you," she said. He denied it. She said she admired his mind – did he understand that? She hadn't ever met a professor before. He was fun to be with. He said such funny things and told her such interesting facts. She didn't want to spoil it.

Harry smiled and said nothing. What was there to say? If she didn't want more than that he wasn't going to complain or argue. He still thought she'd sent out contradictory signals, but he didn't say so.

When the lift arrived she got in with him. Was he sure

he didn't mind? She didn't want to spoil the lovely day they'd had. Did he understand what she meant when she said it was his mind she admired? That she'd never met anyone who was really clever?

It seemed to Harry like half a dialogue, the other half of which would have turned it into a picturesque little lovers" tiff. He had no appetite for such a mundane drama. He supposed his good-humoured silence expressed what he felt – a sort of ironic surprise.

Now they were at his door. She asked would he kiss her goodnight. He said no he wouldn't but he would tell her a bedtime story, which she could take back to her room and think about. Then he told her about Bernard Shaw and the beautiful actress who suggested to Shaw that they should have a child. "With your brains and my beauty," the actress said, "what a child that would be!" "Ah but Madame," Shaw replied, "what if the child should turn out to have my beauty and your brains."

Harry kissed her lightly on the forehead and left her at his door.

Next morning she arrived at breakfast after him. There was no one else at his table, but she didn't sit with him. He ate his breakfast slowly and was still reading the *Straits Times* when she got up to leave. She paused beside him on her way to the door.

"Did you mean I haven't got any brains," she asked.

Harry laughed. "Of course I didn't."

"Well you meant something," she said.

Harry put the paper down. He wondered what he did mean. It was not unconnected with the fact that she'd let him pay for everything yesterday – their lunch, their drinks, the movie. But he wasn't going to tell her that.

"You paid me a compliment," he said. "I returned it. That's all."

She frowned and walked on out of the room.

Harry went back to the *Straits Times.* He felt relieved. The night before he'd been disappointed. A certain excitement had been aroused and then dashed. But now he was glad not to be suffering anxiety, or guilt, or the sense of any responsibility to Mandy Rivers. Now he was going to enjoy Singapore.

On the whole he didn't enjoy it. He found it boring. It seemed to him a big shopping complex on a tropical island, and since he'd never been an enthusiastic shopper it didn't interest him. But what made the day strange was that he kept seeing Mandy Rivers. At first he thought it must be coincidence. Then his sense of statistical probability told him it wasn't. She must be following him. But each time he saw her she behaved as if he was following her. She frowned and turned away. There was something quite fierce about her which he liked, especially because it went along with that little girl voice and a whimsical, slightly batty manner. She'd taken the Bernard Shaw story as an insult, and she wasn't forgetting it.

At last Harry found a street that looked interesting because all at once the high-gloss buildings petered out. He remembered it afterwards as a rutted, dingy road, with quite big private houses along each side. Here the tropical vegetation had the upper hand, and so did the climate. Paint peeled, wood rotted, paving lifted as roots forced their way through, lizards came and went through cracks in the masonry, and a few invisible birds shot strange ugly sounds at your ears as you passed, sniping from behind barricades. Now and then a dog hurled itself against a high iron gate, barking and snarling as he passed. There was no one about except an occasional Chinese amah looking down suspiciously from a balcony. On the empty road there was only Harry, sweating in the intolerable heat, and behind him a figure he could see out of the corner of his eye as he half turned his head to look at the houses. Without looking properly he knew the person following him was Mandy.

It was the middle of the day and he was looking for a lunch that wasn't an American-international or hotel lunch. He came to an open market, simply a space where the yellow-orange soil was beaten flat and over it a roof was supported on pillars, protecting the market stalls from sun or rain. There was a little collection of dingy unsteady tables around a cooking stall, and he sat down and ordered a rice meal. The figure that followed him sat down too, almost directly behind him, so he needed to turn his head to catch sight of her. She too ordered rice.

The cook was an Indian. He threw handfuls of this and that into the rice, scattered coloured powders over it, and tossed it about vigorously in his wok over a gas flame fed from a bottle. There was a dirty bandage around his upper arm and as he worked the bandage came loose revealing a leaking wound. Harry didn't know what his reaction to this might have been if he hadn't felt he was being watched by Mandy. Would he have got up and left? Or would he have told himself, as he did now, that if a few drops from the wound fell into his lunch they would probably be sterilized in the wok? What interested him was to see what Mandy would do. Like him, she sat tight, and when the lunch came she ate it.

He got up first. She was still at her table, looking straight ahead. He was struck, by how pretty she looked sitting there with a sort of grim, baby-faced determination; and also by the fact that she was something more than just "odd". Entirely sane, but somehow removed, exempt from the usual proprieties. A nuisance maybe, but more interesting than Singapore's shopping arcades.

He stopped by her table. "Did you enjoy it," he asked. She said she did.

He said he'd enjoyed it too. More than he'd expected to. Then he said, "You're not offended are you?"

She frowned down at her hands, thinking about it. "I'm not sure," she said. "Probably I am." And then she looked up at him and smiled and said "I think you're a stinker Harry."

That evening they danced again at the hotel. They danced for hours, and drank a beautiful dry white wine and ate oysters off the shell with pepper and lemon and small pieces of brown bread. When it was time to stop she clung to him. A little the worse for wear and for wine, he headed for his room. She could come with him or not, it was up to her. She came. All the way she never let go of his arm. But when they got inside and closed the door her behaviour again seemed strange to him. She didn't at once throw herself into his arms, or act as if they were lovers. She wandered about the room looking at everything. She opened the refrigerator and checked that it contained, as hers did, bottles of every conceivable alcoholic drink and a few non-alcoholic as well. "But you know they replace each one you drink," she told him. "And when you leave they charge you."

Had she been to Singapore before? What was she doing there? He hadn't seemed to have a chance to ask her – she was clever at steering the conversation away from herself. But now Harry didn't care. He moved to take hold of her, but she was gone, into the bathroom.

She was in there a long time. When she came out she turned on the television. She was behaving more like a wife than a new lover. Were they going to make love? Harry had begun to think not. But then, still watching the set, she began to take off her clothes. She did it in a way that was at once absent-minded and practical. Shoes kicked off first. Then dress, pantyhose, bra and knickers, laid over a chair – and all the time her eyes on the set, never on Harry. She kept laughing as if she understood the jokes, but the programme was in Chinese with Malay subtitles. She went on standing there, unselfconsciously watching. Harry leaned back against the table, watching her.

Then she lay down on the bed and looked at him. "O.K." she said. "Fire away."

Lying there in the rubber dinghy that was drifting along the shore-line of Mission Bay, Harry didn't go into a lot of detail about what happened next, and although Phil asked questions he didn't want to seem over-interested in this part of the story. What he gathered was that Harry was at first put off by Mandy's detachment. Making love to her presented itself as something like a confidence course. How was he going to engage her interest, arouse her passion, light her fire? Then gradually he recognized that he wasn't required to do any of these things. If he specially wanted her to be excited, she would pretend. But really there was no need. She was lending him her body. He could enjoy himself with it as much as he liked and more or less in whatever way he pleased. Meanwhile she might be somewhere else – away in her head, or just turning her eyes to that Chinese television with the Malay sub-titles.

And once Harry understood this – that nothing was required of him except just to get on with it and enjoy himself – then what had seemed so daunting turned into something new and different – as piquant and special in its way as those oysters and that beautiful dry white wine.

When it was over and Harry was drifting off to sleep, Mandy asked "What did you mean when you said I paid you a compliment?"

He had to struggle to remember. Then it came back to him – his answer when she had asked whether the Bernard Shaw story was meant to suggest she had no brains.

"You said I was really clever."

"Oh but you are," she said, as if she thought he might doubt it.

"And you're very beautiful," he said.

She thought about this, lying staring at the ceiling. "Yes, but I'm quite clever too," she said.

"And I'm not bad looking," Harry said.

They laughed a lot at that. And then fell into a long silence that was broken by quieter secondary eruptions of laughter. After a while Harry found himself with a new erection.

"I think I'll just do that again," he said.

Mandy moved to accommodate him. "Fire away," she said. And for a few moments she crooned a song to herself, and incidentally to him, because his ear happened to be only an inch from her mouth.

Three or four times during the night Harry half-woke, reached out, ran his hands over her body, and fell asleep again. In the morning he reached out and she wasn't there. He phoned her room but there was no answer. He knocked on the way down. No reply – and she wasn't in the breakfast room either.

Harry was to leave that evening – eight hours on a night flight direct to Sydney. He spent most of the day looking

124

for Mandy. There was no sign of her anywhere, but according to the hotel desk she hadn't checked out.

He thought this was more or less as it ought to be – a night together and then nothing. But of course it wasn't what he wanted. He wanted to see her one more time. Just to say goodbye.

So our final scene has Harry Butler joining a queue to check in his luggage at Singapore airport, looking a bit forlorn maybe, but glad to be going home. When two hands slide under his arms he doesn't have to turn around to see who it is. "Where have you been," he says.

She doesn't really answer his question. She had things to do. She got lost. There were people she had to see. She says a lot and tells him nothing. But now she's leaving with him on the same flight. Isn't that a coincidence!

They check in and go through Customs and Immigration together. In the departure lounge he tells her about the philosophical argument over whether man can build machines which think. Whether the thinking machines do is the same as the thinking that men do. Harry hasn't any doubt about it. They're not the same. The problem is how to prove that they're not.

"A machine that thought like I do would get scrapped," Mandy says.

Harry laughs. "And a man who thought like a machine would get locked up."

As Harry told it to Phil that was pretty well the end of the story. They flew to Sydney together, and Mandy left him at Sydney airport. She was living in Sydney at the time. Harry flew on to Auckland. He never saw her again until she turned out to be the new neighbour next door. He felt nervous about that, but she behaved as if they'd never met, and so did he.

"You never spoke to her," Phil asked.

Harry sat up and began to paddle towards the shore. "Only a nod or so over the fence."

Those were the facts Phil went over in his head. Next day he was on the phone to Harry. He wanted to know more about what happened at Sydney airport. Harry found it difficult to remember. He thought his own luggage must have been checked straight through, but there was a stop of a few hours. He thought he might have helped Mandy through Customs with hers.

"Were you holding her handluggage?"

Harry couldn't remember. "I might have been."

"Has it occurred to you you might have been carrying a handbag that had no labels? One she could deny was hers if it got searched?"

There was a silence while Harry considered. He hadn't thought of it and now that he did it didn't seem likely.

"Why do you think she attached herself to you," Phil asked.

"I think she liked me."

Phil didn't conceal his irritation. "She's living with a drug-pusher. You were set up. You must have been."

"Don't spoil it on me," Harry said. "It's a happy memory."

"You should take it seriously."

"I'll try," Harry said; but he didn't sound serious.

After he'd put down the phone Harry stood looking down at the palm trees in the park. Maybe Phil was right.

The phone rang. It was Phil again. "I think I should warn you, old chum . . ."

"As far as I'm concerned," Harry said, "the drug squad's gone and it's over."

"What you don't know is that Larson has worked

126

out that you were in Singapore with Mandy Rivers."

Harry didn't reply to that.

"And you'd better be quite sure you haven't spoken to her since then," Phil said. "Because Larson thinks you might have warned her they were being watched."

NINETEEN

Trackback: Jason in the Turf Bar

In Rapallo Uta was waiting for me, as arranged, at a seafront café. It was along at the eastern end of the bay, where there wasn't the width of the promenade between the café and the water. "This is where you will write," she said. "Signor Illiano knows already about your important work."

"Please be welcome to my umble café," the padrone said.

Uta had chosen well. The café was quiet, but with views across the water when I wanted to lift my head and look out.

The Hotel Miranda, in which she'd booked me a room, was at the other end of the bay. But she knew I liked a walk before starting work; and that I preferred to keep my living quarters and my place of work separate.

My hotel room was on the first floor. She helped me to open the green wooden shutters, which were threatening to fall to bits, and we stepped out on to the balcony. Directly below there was a little canal. Beyond were phoenix palms, and the town, and the bay. Away to the left was the headland and the church of Sant'' Ambrogio.

Of course I felt a little nervous at having my life so managed by Uta, but I had to admit it was perfect. I felt sure I could work here. And already I'd begun to hear in my head the voice which belonged to the blue folder. Uta gave me a tourist map of Rapallo on which she'd marked a walking path I could take up on to the headland and the road to her house. She thought I might like to be left alone in the mornings. In the afternoons I could walk up and visit her. Of course if I wanted to work up at her house I would be welcome – that was understood. But she knew my preference for writing in cafés.

I gave her a tentative hug as she was leaving. "Thank you Uta," I said. "You've done wonders."

"I've done nothing," she said. "You're the one who must do the wonders."

The Story, lying there in its blue folder on the big bed, seemed already to be talking about Jason. I wanted a shower and a shave, and to relax. I wanted to enjoy this room with its high ornate ceiling, its pink and pale green furniture with curves and swirls in the woodwork which drew to points painted in gold; and out there, through the aging curtains and arthritic shutters, that view of phoenix palms and a glittering sea.

After my shower I found the plug to my electric shaver cord didn't match the fitting over the mirror. With the help of a pair of nail scissors I took the two-pin plug off the bedside lamp and wired it to my razor cord. Then I pushed the bare wires of the lamp into the wall fitting. That way I had a razor which worked without losing my bedside lamp.

"So you're ready," the voice in my head said – the one that speaks for the Story. "Now I suppose we've got to make our way back to the café. And then you'll want to put down something amusing about the padrone."

But I had another idea. I took a chair and the small bedside table out on to the balcony and got ready to begin work at once. This so pleased the Story we worked for a couple of hours, until the light started to fade, with scarcely an angry word or a serious disagreement. What we decided was that we had to go right back to the scene in the Turf Bar when Jason arrived saying he was in the money. But then to explain that properly we had to go back even further. We'd given very little information about Jason; but that was only because there was very little to give. Even Harry and Phil, who'd known him so many years, knew very little about his private life. Of course we could have invented a life, one which probably wouldn't have differed much from the truth. But that would have been dangerous. When you invent you lose confidence. Your tone changes, and the really alert reader (and I suppose it was Uta I had in mind) knows she's no longer getting a truthful account.

I got up from the little table on the balcony and walked around my room, looking at those ornate ceilings and gold arrow-head designs on the woodwork, and the curl shapes on the bed-head and the bedside lamp. I felt sure Jason would have liked this room. "We need a symbol," I said.

"Forget symbols," the Story said. "Just stick to the facts." And it reminded me of one. Jason had been born with the little finger missing from his left hand. As deformities go it was minor – insignificant. People didn't notice it; and Jason took a great deal of trouble to hide it. Once or twice Harry and Phil had spoken of it, but never when Jason was present. Somehow he conveyed this absolute rule that his missing finger wasn't mentioned.

I wanted to comment on this, on what it meant about Jason's character, his sensitivity, his secrecy, and even about the curious force of his personality that could silently make rules to protect itself, but the Story shut me up. "Just the fact," it said. And as if to silence my protest it hurried me through a rapid summary of Jason's life and character.

He always lived well and spent lavishly – that was certainly true. When there was anything to celebrate he celebrated, usually with champagne. He cooked well and liked big dinner parties. He hated gardens and gardening, but he loved to send flowers or to bring them. He liked to arrive by taxi, even when it might have been simpler to walk or to drive his own car. He dressed informally, or it might be more accurate to say unconventionally, but always with style. Even when he turned up – as he did that afternoon at the Turf Bar – wearing the clothes of a working man, there was that red scarf at the throat to put the whole outfit into inverted commas, like a quotation or a caption: "Jason Cook as working man".

After he left the trotting establishment at Takanini he became a sort of prototype small businessman, but one who lived free and never allowed himself to be tied down by his own ambitions and enterprises. For ten years or more money never seemed to be a problem. When he ran out of it he took a job, or invented something, or started a new business. He could have become very rich but he took money for granted. It would always be there when he needed it. His main purpose in life seemed to be to stay free and to keep moving. Life was to be lived and money was to be spent.

Then in the seventies everything changed. Not overnight. It happened gradually, and Jason was probably slow to notice. As long as he could he averted his eyes. But in the end he had to recognize what was happening to him.

He couldn't any longer afford champagne and taxis and flowers and dinner parties. Sources of credit were running out. He'd bought a big house near One Tree Hill and spent a lot of money furnishing it with antiques. Now the antiques began to vanish – first the old piano painted in pale greens and golds with woodland scenes of nymphs and shepherds; then the gold harp that stood in the corner; then the Persian carpets and candelabras. At a certain point it became impossible to sustain the image. The house was sold and replaced by another, more modest. Jason went back to the seagrass matting and Japanese screens, the rattan and ricepaper style of his younger days, more austere, less flamboyant, but even that cost money. He was like a camel living off its hump as it crossed the desert. But how far into the distance did the desert stretch?

This is where the sherry-drinking mother with the shares in South African diamond mines ought to have stepped on to the scene. But there was no sign of her and no word about her. Maybe she'd been a myth. Anyway there appeared to be no family resources to fall back on. Jason made a joke of it. He said he could no longer support himself in the manner to which he was accustomed. But it wasn't a joke. There were times in the Turf Bar when he couldn't buy his round.

All this is background to that scene in the bar. Jason had told them he was in the money and gone to buy his round of drinks. Harry was staring straight ahead, looking as if he'd drunk too much already, and talked too much. This was the day that had begun buoyantly with his statement typed out in capitals for the pin-board: THERE ARE ONLY PHILOSOPHICAL PROBLEMS AT THE POINT WHERE LANGUAGE BEGINS TO FAIL. Since then there had been the visit of the two from the Women's Collective, followed by the scene with Louise Lamont, and then Edith, and after all that an average day for a professor of philosophy who was also head of his Department. By now it seemed to Harry that more than language was failing and that his problems were more than philosophical.

Jason fought his way back from the bar with the drinks, sat down, spread himself. He looked at Harry, at Phil, at Harry again. "Smile you buggers," he said. "This is a celebration."

What must have been on Phil's mind now, and on Harry's, was the question of where the money was coming from and what they were celebrating. They might also have been thinking that they ought to have worked out a strategy for how those questions were to be approached.

It was Harry who found his voice first. "Here's to whatever it is," he said, raising his glass. And then while Jason was taking his first sip, Harry went straight at the problem. "What do you mean by visiting our next-door neighbours and not calling on us?"

Jason hesitated. "Saw me did you? I was in a big hurry that day. No time to stop."

Silence. No questions invited.

"So what are we celebrating," Phil asked.

"Work," Jason said. "Money. Luck."

What he told them was that he'd landed a contract to work on a property on a peninsula north of Auckland. He was to repair the landing jetty, clear the foreshore for a boat-ramp, make a path up through the bush, clear a sight where a pole-house was to be built, and put in the poles. If his employers still liked him at that point, he could contract to build the house. It was hard to get materials in – they had to come over unsealed roads or by sea – and the whole job was left to him. Money no obstacle. Poles in by helicopter. He sent invoices to a box number and they were cleared from there. And as a bonus he got his own payments in cash so they didn't have to be declared to Inland Revenue.

Silence again. Jason looked from one to the other. "Well thanks chaps for that rousing cheer."

Phil asked, "Where do you collect your money?"

"Different places. It comes through a lawyer's office."

"Was that what you were doing next door," Harry asked.

Jason frowned across the table. "Don't you think we could celebrate my bit of luck without an inquisition. It's money and I like it. See?"

Harry said, "As soon as we're sure it's luck we'll be joining you old boy."

"Which means what?"

"You nearly got your face into drug squad files. And it wasn't luck that kept you out."

Jason shook his head. "I don't know what you're talking about." He looked as if he didn't want to know, either, but Phil explained it all patiently – the drug squad in Harry's house, Greg Carey's record. It seemed – at least judging by appearances – that it was all new to Jason. New and unwelcome. He kept shaking his head and frowning. "This is stuff I don't want to know about."

"If you're taking risks you'd better know about it," Harry said.

Again Jason shook his head. "If there's a risk it's probably in knowing. The less you know the better."

The likelihood that this was true silenced Harry for a moment.

"It's easy for you blokes to pick and choose," Jason said. "You're the salary-and-super brigade."

"Stop feeling sorry for yourself," Phil said. "If it's bad money, you need to know that it is."

Jason smiled grimly. "What's bad money? Or good money? It's the same dollar note whatever pocket it's been in. I just want it to go in and out of mine on the way round. I don't see why I need to know where else it's been, any more than you do with yours."

There was a bit of bad feeling now. They drank in silence. "It's that question of luck," Harry said. "It's not morality. The morality's up to you. But if you're in something that gets your mug into police files then it's up to your friends to tell you about it."

"Well," Jason said, "if you put yourself into the line of fire for me, Harry, I'm grateful. I mean I'm grateful for the thought and all that. But you could just be making trouble for me. I've got a clear conscience. I'm being paid good money to do some honest work – and I'm enjoying it. It's great. It's a beautiful place and I'm my own boss. You should come and look at it. Lovely bay, good swimming, fishing, bush, the lot. Bring the kids."

TWENTY

God in Purple and Green

Harry Butler's senior seminar was held in the small carpeted room to which he alone had a key. It was held on
Thursday evenings, the same evening that Claire went to
her weekly session with Duag MacPherson or Abd-bin-
Abdal. A neighbour's daughter was baby-sitter for Jonah
and Reuben. Claire dropped Harry at the university and
drove across town to her class.

The senior seminar wasn't compulsory. It was open to
third and fourth year philosophy students and to those
doing post-graduate work. They sat around in comfortable chairs, drank coffee, and sometimes wine after the
serious discussion was over. Sometimes Harry delivered
himself of his latest thinking on some philosophical subject, or talked about a recently published book, but he
never gave a formal lecture from prepared notes. As he
talked he interrupted himself, or the students interrupted
him, to ask questions. They weren't expected to take notes
– in fact he preferred them not to – but some of them did
because they liked these sessions better than his formal
lectures.

It has to be said that opinion about these performances
of Harry's was divided. Most of his students seemed to
enjoy them. Some of Harry's staff had their doubts and
wondered whether he wasn't showing signs of losing his
grip on his subject.

So we home in on this informal scene in the small

seminar room at a point where someone has introduced the word "soul" into the discussion.

Harry pounces on it. Soul, he tells the group, is a useful word, but if you're going to use it philosophically a lot of care is needed. He suggests to begin with that the word might mean something like the essential and unique identity of a person. The soul expresses itself in thought and language. It also might be thought to express itself in the way a person walks, or moves. Soul, Harry suggests, has style but no opinions.

Someone in the group says it would be hard to distinguish soul from mind.

Harry agrees. It's only a matter of the particular colouration of meaning each word has acquired through usage. You have to be very careful, he tells them, not to think that because there are two words, soul and mind, there are therefore two "things" to match them. There may not even be one "thing". But the word mind suggests something more limited than the word soul. It suggests intellect. Not intellect exclusively, because dreams, imagination, and so on are also attributes of mind. But the word has that emphasis. We tend to think we control our own minds, at least to some extent; and to the extent that we do, our mind is a machine we put to use – the use of thinking, or of imagining. It's distinct from brain, but closely allied to it. Brain is the physical object, or the location. Mind is our sense of having faculties of thinking and knowing and dreaming, whether or not we happen to be aware that the instrument with which this is done is located in the head. And he reminds them that ancient man believed emotions were located in the heart – hence all those metaphors about broken hearts, bleeding hearts, hearts taking flight, heavy hearts.

So we experience the mind in part as an instrument. The soul is something more comprehensive – a more comprehensive and ineffable sense of ourselves. You might say the soul is expressed partly in the way we use our minds.

But all these words are overlayed in meaning, one over another. The word mind lies partly over the word brain, yet it isn't the same and it extends further. In the same way the word soul lies partly over the word mind but extends further. It's no use arguing with one another about whether a soul is this or that – whether it's free, or immortal, or beautiful, or oblong, or orange, or whatever. What we should do is look at the way the word traditionally functions, and this will reveal to us something about our notion of ourselves.

Someone points out that the soul has traditionally been thought of as immortal, and not, incidentally, as orange or oblong.

Harry says he makes a distinction here between what is indispensable in the traditional use of the word, and what you can, if you choose, do without. If you removed the word soul from the language, he says, and didn't allow any other word, like spirit, to replace it, then there would be a gap. The word mind is not quite same as the word soul and so couldn't quite do duty for it. Soul is a word we need because it matches something in our sense of ourselves. Christianity, and other religions as well, have customarily confused the discussion by forcing two words together – "immortal soul". The question is put "Do you believe a human being has an immortal soul?" Since most people have a sense that the word soul expresses something they recognize in their experience, the tendency is to assent. But the word immortal has been slipped in there by sleight of hand. Whether the word soul is meaningful to us, and whether what it means is something which has the property of immortality, are separate questions.

When a questioner looks dissatisfied Harry invites them to consider the case of a person who has suffered what's called "brain death" – irreversible damage so that although the heart is pumping, and the cells of the body are alive, there is no brain function. No brain waves are recorded. Brain is dead, so there is nothing you could call mind operating. Under these circumstances there is no longer any evidence that whatever we mean by soul continues to exist. Traditionally the souls of the dead are thought of as departing from the body. But what of the case of the living dead? Is the soul to be thought of as hanging around in there, a sort of white handkerchief, or a puff of blue smoke, waiting for the signal to take off? This is the stuff for a fantasy by Edgar Allen Poe, rather than for philosophical discussion. Soul, in fact, is an abstraction from actions. Isn't it therefore a logical error to give it an existence separate from those actions which characterize it? Isn't it more reasonable to say that when the action ceases the occasion for abstracting from it ceases also?

A young man wants to know whether Harry is equating Christianity with a fantasy by Edgar Allan Poe.

Harry says what he's trying to show is that you can dispense with the notion of immortality without doing damage to the capacity the language has to express our sense of human life and human experience. Not only that, the notion of immortality can be decidedly awkward. To say that somewhere – or mystically nowhere – within the person suffering brain death there is a soul alive and well is no more than a statement of faith. One might even say, of blind faith. It has a powerful tradition behind it. But there's nothing you can point to in the actual circumstances to support it. You're asked to believe it because it's comfortable, and because others have believed it before you.

The young man says he thinks Harry is trying to remove the mystery from human life.

On the contrary, Harry says. The mystery is in our consciousness of ourselves and in the limits of that consciousness, and the limits of the language in which it has to be expressed. It's the traditional religions which have removed the mystery by claiming to explain the inexplicable. Who made us? God. What happens when we die? We go somewhere else. How can we do that? Because a part of us, called the soul, which is invisible, is also immortal. Only when a frown of doubt crossed the Christian forehead did the ancient fathers of the church begin to talk about the mystery. Having removed the mystery, they pretended to put it back again. What they called the mystery was the bits left over, the ragged edges of doubt, where the traditional explanations left the hearer dissatisfied. God works in mysterious ways, they said. But that was the mystery which God had been invented to remove.

Louise, sitting on a table near the back, says "Aren't you getting away from the point, Harry?"

Harry hesitates. "I'm never sure in these sessions that there is a point. Or that there ought to be." He looks around the group. "Do you want to leave God out of it?"

There is a general shaking of heads. After a moment someone says "Isn't God one of those words like soul that would leave a gap in the language if you removed it?"

Harry thinks about this. He says it is and it isn't. When he talked about the word soul representing something in our sense of ourselves he meant that it has its own quite distinct and subtle shade of meaning, different from brain and even from mind. The word God on the other hand – God with a capital G – has no such subtlety or precision. In fact it's all things to all men.

"And women," one of the Philosophy Department Women's Collective interrupts.

A group of people could be talking about God, Harry goes on. One could say I see God as the father and creator of all things. A second could say no to that anthropomorphic old-man-in-the-skies stuff and argue that God is everywhere and everything – the spirit of the created universe. A third could say he sees God as standing aloof and indifferent outside His own creation. A fourth could say God's job was to hand out rewards and punishments. A fifth could say that God was a fence post. A sixth that God was the primal atom. And so on. Almost the only agreement is that God is powerful, and possibly that he's in some way responsible for everything – but even those attributes are subject to argument. No word illustrates better how language can trap us. If a word gets into circulation and gets used a lot, we behave as if there must be something it refers to. It's a bit like setting up a fund-raising committee and then looking around for a charity to give the money to.

Harry is asked whether he's an atheist or an agnostic.

He says it's a trap to say you have to be either theist, atheist, or agnostic, because each of these positions lends a certain respectability to the word God. The theist believes in God. The agnostic isn't sure. The atheist doesn't believe in God. But which God? Each of these positions implies the meaning of the word God is intelligible – even though the believers may be murdering one another over how God should be properly described and worshipped. Harry says he prefers to stay right out of that linguistic mess and keep his boots clean.

Someone suggests he has evaded the question. What is he if he's neither theist, nor atheist, nor agnostic?

Harry replies that he's a non-theist, and he insists, against some sceptical murmuring, that it's a perfectly proper description. To the question "Do you believe in God?" his answer would have to be "I can't answer because I don't understand the question." That's not, he says, evasion. It's precision.

The woman from the Collective says the language – or the grammar – of Harry's examples reveals a sexist bias. He has made a few feeble attempts to shake off his bad linguistic habits, but more than once he has referred to the people in his examples as "he", as if only the thinking that men do is of any interest.

Harry bridles. He says grammatical bullying by feminists is the most conspicuous form of sexual harassment in the university.

The young woman isn't deterred. She says the real point about traditional notions of God is that they're male. They are sanctions for a male power structure.

Harry says that's a different debate. If God had traditionally been female, and there had been a female power structure – a matriarchy – all the statements he has made about the word God would still hold true.

In Duag MacPherson's Herne Bay sitting room, cleared of its furniture, the group sat around on cushions. They'd spent the past few minutes in silence and now they were comparing the colours that had come into their minds. Claire Butler, trying hard to be Sophia, had seen purple edged with green.

"What do you associate with that colour," Duag Mac-Pherson asked her.

She thought a moment. "I think possibly sex," she said. He made no comment.

After a further silence he began to address the group again. He said that the traditional notion of the *jihad* – the holy war – was a real shooting war only in its crudest and least interesting form. The *jihad* was purest when it went on inside the soul of man. It was the war against the ego, and against the ego's instrument, the body. The soul's colours would never be clear while the ego stood against the light.

"There is a hunger in all our hearts," he said, "for the pure colours of God to be registered. We hunger for that light which comes from eternity, but the ego and the appetites stand perpetually in the way. Yet at the same time that this is true it's also true that there is no one right way to the light, no certain and infallible path to the truth. Each must find his own. That's why our minds have to be open to every possibility, even some which may on the face of it surprise us or shock our conventional notions of propriety. Fasting is good for the body, and the soul certainly craves the liberation it brings. Faith, prayer, fasting, almsgiving and pilgrimage are traditionally the five pillars of Islam. Yet there's always the possibility God may come to us in a good old kiwi pie."

He smiled around at them. "What each of you knows by now is that we are all day by day putting together a straw man, a puppet, a tailor's dummy, which we push forth into the world and to which we attach our own names. 'That's me,' we say – Duag MacPherson, or Jamie Reid, or Claire Butler, or Indu Sophira. That self is false. We construct it out of fear and out of pride and out of base appetite. Some of you will know some of the poetry of T. S. Eliot, one of the few Christian poets who was not blind to the subtler wisdoms of the east. In one of his poems Eliot writes about fear, and about 'preparing a face to meet the faces that you meet'. Those prepared faces are the masks we all wear. They hide ourselves from ourselves. They shield us from the colours of eternity. I don't suppose they hide us from God, but I think God smiles and says nothing and looks the other way. He has time on his side. Mostly God seems content to wait. But He's also unpredictable. Remember the possibilities of the kiwi pie, and be ready to take them whenever and wherever they're offered. There is Grace as well as prayer and fasting, and Grace is a shortcut anyone should welcome, because mostly the road is long and hard, the climate harsh, and the burden heavy. Our purpose is to discover the Real. You come to me because you've had, as I have had at intervals throughout my life, a sense of the agony of feeling that everything around you is without meaning, even without reality. That happens when the colours of eternity are lost. The sun may be in the sky and the grass may be growing under our feet, but the world dies for us at those moments. The wisdom of the Sufi tells us there is no reality without *the* Reality. Only when the colours of eternity are allowed into our souls does the world regain meaning and value for us. In our negative moments – or they may be days, or years – we have to cling to that truth stated by the Hindu saint Ramakrishna when he said 'God and His name are One'. When all else fails we can at least utter His name. That is our last card, our ultimate resource. The name of God is the mantra of mantras, because it is God Himself who invokes, God Himself who is invoked, and God Himself who is the invocation."

144

Harry locked the small seminar room. Along the corridor he could hear the students in the common room kitchen. He took his bag from his desk, switched off the lights, and locked his office. He went towards the lifts but then changed his mind and walked down a flight of stairs to the fourth floor. The door to the study Louise Lamont shared with two other post-graduate students was ajar and the light was on. He put his head into the room. She was standing behind her desk, sorting papers. She looked up at him but she didn't speak. There was an awkward silence. Always after his seminars she said something about his performance – "You were good tonight", or just a pat on the back as they clustered around the sink making coffee. It was ridiculous, he knew, but he looked for that approbation.

"Everything all right," he said.

"Yes." She looked at her papers again. Then she said, "No of course it isn't."

He came through the door and half-closed it behind him. "What's the matter?"

She still held one sheaf of papers in her right hand and stared at them. "Nothing's the matter really. It's just I promised I'd tell you if anything like this happened. Matthew Holden came around at the weekend. I went to bed with him."

Harry looked as if his limbs had gone heavy. That was how it felt. He sat down very slowly.

"It was raining," Louise said.

He nodded. "We had a flood." There was what seemed a long silence. Louise solved some problem with the papers.

"Good, was it," Harry asked.

She looked at him directly for the first time. He had the

sort of face that registered pain precisely, even when he was trying to conceal it. She looked away.

"Enjoyed yourself, did you," Harry said.

Her almond eyes, that might have been softening, hardened. "It's difficult not to enjoy an orgasm isn't it Harry? Don't you find that with your wife?"

He got up, clutching his bag, and made his way out. Looking at his back, as Louise did, you might have thought the bag was full of stones.

"Harry," she said, but not so he could hear.

Ten minutes later Claire pulled up in the Porsche in Princes Street. She offered him the keys but he shook his head. "You drive," he said.

Claire glanced at him as they stopped at a traffic light on their way down to the waterfront. "How did it go? Hard work?"

"About average," he said. "No. Worse than average. I got on to God again."

"You should leave God to people who've been there."

Harry shook his head. "They're the ones you can't trust. Too much special pleading. How was the carpet seller?"

"He was good tonight," Claire said. "I wasn't."

"What went wrong?"

"I don't think I'm getting the right colours." She glanced to see whether he was with her. "In my head."

"What colours are you getting?"

"Of the flesh, I think."

He nodded. "Can't be all bad."

"It's not what we aim for you know."

"How will you know when you get it right?"

"I'm not sure. I imagine I'll know all right. Abdal said tonight God might come to us in a pie."

"That's how He comes to me," Harry said. "With tomato sauce."

"You don't eat pies."

"I steer clear of Him if I can. He's bad for someone in my line of work."

They drove along the waterfront in silence. When they reached Mission Bay she turned into the carpark and pulled up at the sea wall. They sat staring out at the lights on the water. After a while Claire said, "Are you unhappy?"

He said "No." Then he said, "Well maybe."

"Is it me," Claire asked. "Am I the problem?"

He shook his head. "I'm the problem. I'm my problem. You're yours."

She took his hand in both of hers and patted it thoughtfully. "Do you want to divorce me?"

He shook his head again. "No. Do you want to divorce me?"

"No," Claire said. And then she said, "Not often."

He leaned over and kissed her. "Purple and green," she said.

He patted her knee. "Let's go home and have a pie."

TWENTY-ONE

Harry and the Last Hay

Everything moves more slowly than one would like. I've been in Rapallo more than a week, and I like it, the Story seems reasonably satisfied, the writing continues, whether well or badly is something I don't ask myself. But it's a long slow process. Every morning the padrone says "Please be welcome to my umble café". It's a line he has learned – his only piece of English. He doesn't interrupt me as my Milanese padrone did, and I suppose that's good, but it increases my sense of isolation. Uta has been busy up at the house, but we've twice had a meal together on the seafront in the evening.

This morning, however, there's a message for me to phone her as soon as I reach the café. She has at last got around to reading my recent chapters and she wants me to come up to the house at once. I would prefer to work first and come up in the afternoon, but she insists I mustn't write another word until I've talked to her. Of course I resent her interference and her Nordic high-handedness, but she has a certain power over me. I don't forget the Story's absolute silence when she left Milan and came down to the coast.

So I drink a cup of coffee and look over some notes in a gesture of weak defiance, and then I set off up the salita – the cobbled walking path that slants through the olive groves, all the way up to the church of Sant" Ambrogio on the headland above the town. Beyond the church I strike the road again, and walk east towards the cliffs of Zoagli. Uta's house is off to the left, above the road. At the iron gate I ring and at once there's the sound of something like a wolfhound up at the house, baying for blood. Uta's voice comes through on the intercom. I identify myself and she springs the latch on the gate by remote control, at which the sound of the ferocious dog (some kind of electronic device) is switched off.

The house, which must once have belonged to a small farmer, has been beautifully redesigned. You enter at the lower level, where the floors are of blue and white marble and the stone arches are whitewashed. From there you climb a stone stair to the main living room, which in turn opens on to a terrace. At one end of the living room there's a dining table. At the other end a large wooden olive press, some hundreds of years old, has been left in place.

Uta suggests we sit out on the terrace. The day is mild for the time of year, and we sit at a little white iron table, looking down through that smoky light over the olives to the blue-grey sea. It seems to me Uta is agitated, but trying to remain calm. Something in the recent chapters has upset her – I can see that. She makes her way towards it obliquely at first; but she has no talent for southern indirection, and gives it up.

It's difficult to say whether Uta is attacking me or Harry Butler. It's almost as if we are the same person. His Singapore adventure has particularly angered her. She says she doesn't much like it that he has a mistress. It's not fair to Claire and it's not fair to the mistress. Uta considers Harry to be selfish and self-serving and self-indulgent. But she can accept that because after all it's not unusual – probably the majority of men are like that. But this Singapore adventure is the last hay.

149

Uta's English is pretty good so there's confusion for a few seconds while we sort out that by the last hay she means the last straw. I explain to her that it comes from the saying "It's the last straw that breaks the camel's back."

"So it's the last straw," she says. "And this camel has had enough of your Harry Butler."

She tells me she can see him through. She knows his type. There are men who go after women like hunters after game. Every woman is a trophy, stuffed and put on the wall.

I tell her she's exaggerating. Harry's first marriage broke up, but that happens to a lot of people. The Singapore incident was something quite isolated from the rest of his life. He wasn't to know the girl would turn up next door, and then be the subject of a drug squad investigation. Of course his affair with Louise Lamont is quite different. Maybe it's deplorable – if that's how Uta feels about it then I accept that. But my job is to present it as it was. As I've told her before, I don't want to defend Harry. I want to represent him. If Uta can say she recognizes him, then I've done my job.

"But how can you avoid judging," she asks. "I think the facts speak for themselves."

There I can agree with her. The facts speak for themselves. "But they have to be allowed to speak," I tell her. "And you have to allow that they will speak differently to different people."

Uta doesn't think so. Some facts maybe, but not all. Not even most. People know right from wrong. Take that Mandy for example. What kind of a creature must she be? Living with a drug pusher. Carrying drugs from one country to another.

"Do you know the effects of drug-taking," she asks me.

"Do you know what it does to young people? How it destroys first their minds and then their bodies. How can you treat it lightly?"

I tell her I do know these things and I don't treat them lightly . . .

That's as far as I get because now Uta has remembered something else. She has got up suddenly from her chair and walked to the edge of the terrace where she stands with her back to me, her arms folded around her bosom. "And that Singapore sex scene," she says. "I found it disgusting."

This surprises me. I thought there wasn't much sex in that "sex scene" as she calls it – certainly less than Danes are said to accept, even on public television. But then it becomes clear that what has disgusted her is Mandy's indifference, and Harry's willingness to make love to a woman who is not emotionally engaged. "What sort of a woman is that," she asks. "And what sort of a man?"

Once again I try to explain that I don't mind if that's her reaction. Only she has to allow that others will respond differently.

"How is it possible to respond differently," she wants to know.

I'm struggling now. Uta is so forceful. But I say that maybe there's a sort of generosity in the way Mandy made herself available. And a kind of simplicity. Even practicality.

"Huh," Uta explodes, "I find that wealthy" – and there's a further moment of confusion until we sort out that she wishes to say she finds it rich. She finds it rich because it seems Mandy was simply using Harry. She wanted to bring something through Customs without getting caught.

151

I point out that that was Phil Gardner's theory. I admit it's mine too, but it may not be right.

"I think it's right," Uta says.

"Well maybe. It's not possible to be sure. But as for Mandy's detachment – it's possible she had a habit. I mean a drug habit. They say it turns you off . . ."

"You mean this Mandy was a drug addict?" Uta is shocked. "So the professor of philosophy went to bed with a drug addict. That's nice. That's very nice. What kind of philosophy is that? He should lose his job. He's not fit to be in charge of young persons."

I try to explain that this is only a theory of mine. I don't know whether it's true or not. But somewhere in the story Harry refers to Mandy's "pin-point eyes". And isn't there something about her scratching her arms? These could be signs of drug addiction. But on the other hand there are perfectly ordinary ways in which they could be explained.

Uta returns to her chair. She sits silent, looking down through the olives towards the sea. She seems to be trying to understand, and all at once I'm conscious again that I'm very fond of her. I try to guess her age – maybe early thirties. She's tall and has the figure of a young athlete, except that it's hard to imagine a branch of athletics in which that bosom wouldn't be a nuisance. I resist an impulse to reach out and touch her.

"Couldn't we know some of these things for certain," she asks.

I tell her I don't have answers to everything. And then there's the Story's habit of letting things out bit by bit. I have to respect that. I can't for example say whether Mandy took drugs because I don't know. I just have to recognize it's a possibility, and also that it's a possibility

152

that doesn't seem to have occurred to Harry at the time all this was going on.

"He's a bit of a devil, this Harry," Uta says. And for a moment she looks at me almost affectionately. "All those women."

I begin to repeat myself. Two marriages. A mistress. An irrelevant night or two in Singapore. It doesn't seem to me to add up to very much when you spread it out over the forty-odd years of Harry Butler's life. But Uta reminds me of the "old English saying" (as she calls it): Where there's smoke there's fire. And she reminds me it has been said more than once that Harry had a reputation. Am I asking her to believe that those four women are the sum total of Harry's sex life? She thinks they are only the tip of his iceberg.

"Would you like lunch," she asks.

So we have lunch at the big table in the room with the olive press. She gives me pickled herrings and a salad, with Danish bread and Danish beer. It makes a change after the Italian food I've grown used to. She tells me about life at the Consulate, and about their house in Denmark which she's keen to get back to. Over a second beer she returns to the subject of Harry Butler. What she wants to know is whether Claire knew anything about the Singapore incident.

It's a question which makes me recognize again that I fear Uta's disapproval. It's as if she has the power to decide Harry is an unworthy subject and that the whole project must stop. But I'm also afraid of lying to her. So I admit that Claire did find out what happened in Singapore. I admit what's worse, that there was no need for her to find out, and that she did only because Harry dropped hints and then, when challenged, confessed. In some way, it seems, he wanted her to know. Maybe it was just because at that time he was in the habit of telling her everything that happened to him, and he felt uncomfortable carrying around a piece of his life that was a secret from her. Or if that seems too charitable, it might be more plausible to suggest he felt guilty and wanted to be told it didn't matter. Or (worse still) maybe there was some childish desire to boast.

Whatever way you explain it there's no doubt that Harry (and here I try to divert Uta's attention by offering a variety of "old English sayings') spilled the beans, blew the gaff, and let the cat out of the bag.

Uta ignores these linguistic riches. She has gone a trifle frosty again. She wants to know what was Claire's reaction.

I explain that this happened before Claire had gone very far down the Sufi road towards detachment. She reacted as you might say "normally". In other words there was a scene.

"Tell me about this scene," Uta says.

I don't want to tell her about it, but I feel there's no escape, so in a moment of indifference to the consequences (after all, it might be good to be released from this difficult business of writing) I give her a brief and brutal account of it – maybe more brutal even than it was in reality. I leave out the warm-up and go straight to the climax.

Claire accuses Harry of being frivolous, half-baked, egotistical and shallow.

Harry tells her she's all "flower-power and let-it-all-hang-out-man" until put to the test and then she's just another suburban housewife.

Claire says he has brains and genitals but no guts and no heart.

154

He says she might have exactly the opposite deficiency.

She tells him he's a poor advertisement for higher education.

He tells her she's a poor advertisement for higher thought.

She asks why he didn't stay in Singapore with his whore.

He says he doesn't know, he wishes he had.

After a few more exchanges of that order she picks up a manuscript of something he has been trying to write on the old Mind/Body problem and tears it up.

At that he goes to the shrine, takes from it her first figurine (it will later be replaced by a better one) of the whirling dervish, and puts it through the carrot grinder.

She's so angry she comes up behind him and breaks a plate over his head, at which he kicks in a glass panel of the back door and leaves the house.

It's a deplorable scene, one I've hoped to keep concealed, especially from Uta. But when I look at her, waiting for the blow, or blows, to fall on me and on Harry, I see that her expression is neutral. She's thinking while she eats an olive. She might even be mildly amused. At last she shrugs. "I think they loved one another," she says. It's the first time she has admitted such a thing.

So there's another long silence and then she says, "That makes it harder to understand his affair with Louise and hers with God."

"A sort of seven-year itch," I suggest.

Uta half shakes her head. "Maybe." She looks at me. Her ice-blue eyes are strangely heart-warming at this moment. "If everything could be explained," she says, "nothing would be interesting."

Yes – and Uta has given me something new. Not an

explanation, but another light on my subject, a different angle of vision from which it's possible to see that Claire too was having an affair – an affair with God, involving even a change of name.

Uta makes a lethal brew of coffee. Something in me responds to the aroma of it as she pours it into the wide strong white cups. I recognize my growing addiction and she reminds me that the Corso Magenta padrone used to call me "Maestro Balzac" because Balzac died of drinking too much black coffee while writing.

She sits opposite me and sips thoughtfully, holding the cup to her lips and peering at me over the top of it. If I didn't know her better I would think there was something coquettish about that expression.

She asks whether Claire ever connected the Mandy next door with the girl in Singapore. I say she didn't, so I suppose Harry must have confessed to his infidelity without getting around to naming the girl. I suppose the confession blew up suddenly into a row, and after that they never talked about it. But one of Larson Snow's correct guesses (not the only one) was his explanation of the gap in the photograph album. As Larson supposed, there was a crowd scene with Mandy somewhere in the foreground, and Harry removed it from the album when she turned up as their next-door neighbour.

And how long, Uta wants to know, did Mandy and Greg Carey remain at number 27 after the drug squad left?

I tell her it was only about a fortnight. One morning they were gone. It was as sudden as that. No sign of carrier trucks or packing. Just the ranchsliders wide open, things lying about on the floors, the wind blowing through and the white gauzy curtains billowing out over the sun-deck. The lights were on in all the rooms. It seemed Mandy and

Greg had thrown their things together in the middle of the night and taken off.

Uta walks down to the gate with me. She unlocks it and stands back to let me through. "So you think I should carry on with it," I ask.

She smiles and quotes the Corso Magenta padrone. "Let 'em have it, Maestro." She's standing slightly above me on the path, and she leans forward and plants a brief kiss on my forehead. She has never done such a thing before. The kiss feels like a small benediction. But something else touches me more directly. It's that bosom of hers, inadvertantly, momentarily, resting its bulk against my upper arm.

I'm already through the gate but I turn back, hearing myself mumbling something urgent and incoherent about having been very much alone during these months of writing. At the same time I hear the firm strong click of the gate locking, and I find myself looking at her through black iron bars.

"Courage," she says. And then, because I suppose I look wimpish, and full of mute appeal, she adds rather more severely, "Get on with it."

I stumble down the cobbled salita. I've never known the light under the olives to look stranger. How can a light be at once bright, and blue-grey? I pick up a seed fallen from a blue-gum that hangs over the path, and I squeeze it to bring out the scent. Back in my hotel room I put it on the heater, and soon an aroma of eucalyptus pervades the room. As I stand out on my balcony above the canal, looking over the waterfront towards the headland of Sant' Ambrogio, I can smell it distinctly, wafting out into the afternoon air.

TWENTY-TWO

Maxie and Les and the Letter

Louise Lamont in her Mt Eden kitchen at seven thirty or eight in the evening was trying to behave like a modern young woman in command of herself. On the coffee table in the next room lay a letter from Harry Butler which she was trying not to re-read. She'd forced herself to eat something. Now she was doing the dishes with the radio on Hauraki, turned up loud. Before she'd wandered out to the letterbox and found the letter, Matthew had rung. She'd told him not to come – she was working. Her real reason had nothing to do with work. It was because she found him boring. He seemed incapable of conversation. He always wanted to go straight to bed, and then everything happened too quickly. Then he seemed incapable of staying in bed. He got restless, got up, got going – but to do what?

Now that she'd found the letter she wished she had asked him to come.

The letter was Harry at his subtle best. It made her hate him. He began by telling her how wonderful their affair had been – all in the past tense. Then he said they had to stop seeing one another for a while – he suggested six weeks. He told her it was too one-sided. She made it too easy for him. If he could have his wife and family and Louise as well, and all that without disruption, what incentive was there to change anything? She couldn't be content with that, stretching away into the future. He didn't want to lose her; but he couldn't conceal from himself that everything was arranged to suit his convenience. They met when he was free. It was kept secret to suit him. He had a wife, and Louise had to accept that, yet he grew jealous if she went near another man. It was ridiculous. He wanted her to have a better life than that. He was conventional enough to think she should have a marriage and children – not at the expense of a career, if she wanted both, but as well. The thought that their relationship might have to end made him unhappy. He still hoped they would find some way to stay friends. But it had to be different. Something had to change so that she got a better share of the deal. They couldn't go on like this. It was doing no harm to him, but it was standing in the way of a better life for her. Sex was what made it impossible for them to act rationally. They had only to be alone together in a room and the chemistry began to work. Everything else was forgotten. And once that had happened they were tied even closer. Couldn't she see that she had to do something to save herself . . .

So it went on. Harry was nothing if not fluent. It was all true, she supposed. But who asked Harry Butler to act as her saviour? If she'd wanted a saviour she would have gone looking for one. Louise Lamont was in love with him. Even at this moment, hating him, she knew it was true. If he knocked at the door now she would be happy. Until he knocked there would be a cloud of discontent in her sky, and from time to time it would block out the sun.

That was why she hated him. Because if he had loved her in the same way he wouldn't have written her a letter full of concern about her future. He would have been knocking at her door, providing one.

159

Yet that was something she wavered on. For her it was easy to be unequivocal, to let passion rule. She had no one else. She had only to think of him when he was under pressure, pulled two ways – how it showed in his face – and she felt sorry for him.

So as well as hating Harry she shed tears, and looked at his photograph, and even added another couple of rows to the sweater she was knitting him which she would never be able to give him because he wouldn't be able to say where he'd got it. So she might give it to her father. Or wear it herself around the flat. But it was Harry's sweater.

A modern young woman, a research student, politically aware, conscious of the historical role of the female in Western society – such a person didn't sit around knitting sweaters for a man who kept her locked up in a secret compartment of his life to be taken out and used when it suited him. Above all she didn't weep tears into the pattern. Louise knew that. It was theory – good, sound theory. But she wanted to say "Fuck to the theory", because the practice had swamped her. She did say it; but she also threw down the knitting and paced about the room, stopping now and then to look at herself in the mirror.

She wanted Harry now – wanted him physically – and she thought of phoning Matthew and keeping her eyes shut. Would that be a kind of liberation? Would she ever want Matthew as she wanted Harry? Of course it was possible. It was only that she didn't want to want him. Harry was trying to release her from that. He was trying to let her out of her cage. Well thank you Harry Butler (she was angry again now) but she'd rather hoped he would come inside with her, not push her out into the world. Harry the Liberator. Emancipator of the Slaves.

160

But why had he made her a slave if it was only to set her free?

Again something like logic rebelled. How could Harry have made her a slave if she hadn't wanted it? She'd been flattered at first just to have the admiration, and the attentions, of the professor, the Head of Department. Then he'd turned out to be human as well – witty, and imaginative, and tender, and a good lover. She'd felt so strong and bold at first. It had done great things for her confidence, which hadn't in any case been lacking. Now she felt as though all that was gone. Here she was wanting to prostrate herself – ready, almost, if he'd come to the door, to weep and plead. Louise couldn't imagine life without Harry.

When the knock came at her door her heart hardly missed a beat. She knew it wasn't Harry. His knock, like everything else about him, seemed to Louise quite distinctive. Firm, audible, but not assertive. And always just three clear raps. This present knock was like a sort of hammering, as with the side of the fist.

When Louise opened the door and looked out into the darkness she thought she saw two boys – not fully grown – in overalls. Then she saw it was two young women.

"Do you just answer your door to anyone who knocks," one of them asked. "You should be more careful. There've been a number of assaults on women in this area."

At the same time they were coming in. "D'you mind if we talk to you for a minute," one of them said.

Louise recognized them, although she didn't know them well. They were members of the Philosophy Department Women's Collective. She saw them often around the corridors of the Department sticking up posters headed

161

"Women need Women". They both wore their hair cut spiky short. They were often in boots and blue jeans, or as now, overalls and T-shirts. They were about the same height – not much more than five feet – and one had lately put on a lot of weight so her overalls seemed to balloon out, up from the ankles at the back and down from the neck at the front.

They stuck out their hands at Louise. "Les," the first one said, and the second said "Maxie", as Louise shook their hands saying that she was Louise.

Les did the talking. She moved about the room, using a sort of bold boy's voice, louder than necessary, accompanying it with violent, or at least rough, movements of hand and head, like an actress playing the part of Rosalind pretending to be a boy in *A Midsummer Night's Dream*. She was concerned at first about the way Louise had answered her door without looking out to check who was knocking. She wanted to know whether Louise had taken a self-defence course, and whether she belonged to the local Neighbourhood Support Group.

"I'm quite tall," Louise said defensively.

Les and Maxie both shook their heads. "You've got to know where to hit them," Les said. And she did some chopping movements with her hands and an upward swing with the knee with a speed and precision that were impressive.

They promised to add Louise to their list. Someone from the area would be in touch with her.

Louise didn't have the heart to tell them she didn't feel afraid and didn't want lessons in self-defence nor to join a Neighbourhood Support Group.

But now Les was explaining that they'd come to talk to her about a survey that was being done by a coalition of women's groups that had been formed at the university. The campaign against sexual harassment was really gaining momentum. The teaching staff, since they were mostly male, were being obstructive. The administration people were pretending to help but doing nothing.

"What we need is some hard evidence," Maxie said. Her voice, issuing from a severely frowning face, was curiously clear and bell-like.

"There's the Hot-and-Cold Lecturers File in Womenspace," Les said. "We get most of our information from that. We've targetted the lecturers and professors who need sorting out. But that information comes in anonymously from victims. We want to push it further and make an example of a few of these creeps. You can only take undercover action so far. You can paint their names up around the place but you can't get them sacked. What we need is a few women ready to stand up and give evidence to a committee."

What Louise felt was something like fear. "Yes," she said.

There was an awkward pause. "Well," Les said, ruffling her spiky hair with a sudden jerky movement of the hand. "We thought you might help."

"I haven't complained," Louise said.

"No you haven't." Les and Maxie knew that. "But don't you think it's time you did?"

"What am I supposed to complain about?"

Les and Maxie looked at one another. They seemed uncertain how to proceed. Finally Maxie shrugged as if it was obvious. "About harassment."

"In general," Louise asked.

"In particular," Les said. And her face hardened. "Don't you know that if you protect these men you just make it

163

easy for them to strike again. You may be able to cope with it. One of your sisters won't be so lucky. She'll leave the university. Or maybe have a nervous breakdown."

"Well, let her complain," Louise said.

"So you won't help us."

"I told you. I've got nothing to complain about. And I don't approve of the Hot-and-Cold Lecturers File. It's just an invitation for women to slander men they don't like and get away with it because it's anonymous."

"You know why it has to be anonymous," Les said. "But O.K. Let's not get into that argument. We're not asking for anything anonymous. We're asking will you tell a university committee on harassment your experiences with a member of staff."

"A particular member of staff? Or would just anyone do?"

Les stared at her. "You know who we're talking about, Louise. You're not Harry Butler's first victim and you won't be his last unless we can do something about it."

"I'm not anyone's victim," Louise said. "And I love Harry Butler." It came out so instantly and unexpectedly it brought tears to her eyes, which she tried to suppress.

Les and Maxie came closer, looking to comfort her. She shook her head and turned away from them. A moment later the phone rang. She let it ring a while. Then she blew her nose and went to answer it.

It was Harry. He was worrying. Did she understand his letter? He hated writing it but he couldn't think what else to do. She had to have a life of her own – and he began to go over it all again, repeating what he'd said in the letter.

Louise cut across him. "For fuck's sake Harry. You want everything. You want to write a letter like that and then you want me to be pleased."

164

"I'm sorry," he said.

"And don't sound so abject. You're not abject so don't pretend to be. You're sorting out the world to suit yourself, as you always do. Well that's O.K. I admire your strength. But stop kidding yourself it all happens despite you. I despise that."

"You despise me," Harry said.

"No I don't. I just hate your guts. Now fuck off and leave me alone."

And she hung up, returning to the living room where she knew the two in overalls must have heard it all. She walked past them to the door and opened it. "And you fuck off too," she said. "When I want a pair of dykes to do my thinking for me, I'll let you know."

She was surprised at how quickly they went, without even returning the insult, though Les's face had gone hammer-hard under its spikes.

From the door she watched while they pulled on their helmets, climbed on to a powerful motorbike, and roared off into the darkness.

She felt better now. She took up the knitting, pulled it off its needle, and began to pull it undone. After a couple of rows she changed her mind and threaded it back on to the needle.

Louise Lamont knitted, watching television with the sound turned down.

It might have been half an hour later that she thought to look for Harry's letter. It was gone from the coffee table. She searched for it on the floor, in the kitchen, in the bedroom. Everywhere. It was gone. She didn't have any doubt where.

TWENTY-THREE

The Butler, the Gardener and the Cook

There hasn't been a lot of work for the camera team, but here's something they can do. Let's set them again at about nine thirty in the morning on that lower slope of Albert Park, pointing their camera up through the fountain towards the university. The December sun cuts through the arcs of the fountain producing the watermetal effect already described. We zoom in (it might be necessary to use a boom) on the drive between the university Registry and the Library building. Out of the drive comes the Porsche. It hesitates crossing the pavement through pedestrians, turns right, and roars away down Princes Street. Now we have only to swing our camera about and in a minute or two we pick it up again, below us now, going down Bowen Avenue toward Queen Street.

Somewhere down there Harry picks up Phil who's waiting for him on a convenient corner, and they're away, towards the waterfront, and then west to the harbour bridge. Here we need two teams, or one taking the same shot from different angles. I would show the bridge from a long way off – that side-on view that makes it look a slim elegant structure. And then the view of it from Point Erin looking straight into the lanes of traffic, making it appear broad, massive and steep.

Let's also send the lens off to the right to show the bristling forest of masts in the Westhaven marina. Harry and Phil will look down there too as the Porsche climbs the slope of the bridge. Both of them know that somewhere in there is Macready's yacht, *Perdita*, winner of some big races in its day, possibly the Sydney to Hobart race, possibly the Auckland to Suva race – a beautiful ocean-going keeler now retired like a racehorse, "put out to grass" (this is Phil's joke), and rumoured to have made at least once the long trip to Thailand and back.

Next maybe a shot from the Porsche itself. They've reached the bridge summit and they're descending on the north shore side. There's Big Shoal Bay to the right, straight ahead the ridge of Takapuna, and looking over the ridge like a head looking over a fence, the summit of Rangitoto. As they descend the slope the head sinks, like a setting sun or moon, behind the ridge, and finally vanishes.

Now we put our camera among toi toi on the slopes a mile or so from the bridge along the edge of the motorway. Through the feathery heads you hear and then see the Porsche gathering speed. Have we ever given it a colour? I see it now as a sort of burnished noncolour, somewhere between grey and silver, with a hint of something like purple or navy depending on how the light falls – more a metallic shine than a colour, just as the sound of the engine is more a rumble than a note.

And why not an answering shot from the Porsche, looking up the slopes at the toi toi in two uniforms, one white, the other pale mauve, a pampas army marching against the sky?

Phil and Harry might be singing – a raucous hymn, or one of the popular songs of their youth – the sort of noise you make when you're leaving things behind. They're heading north out of town. The engine is warming up, the

167

mild early-summer air is racing over the crook of Harry's elbow, the passing landscape is doing swoops up and swoops down wearing a predominant green patched only occasionally with brown.

The next shot is for contrast. After action, stillness. After noise, this silence. They've stopped the car and they're looking down at a river, its seaward flow stalled by the incoming tide, a sort of brimming reflective stalemate, as in a Japanese print, with cabbage trees standing out on the rutted slopes practising hand signals, all elbows and arms. This is their particular bit of New Zealand. It's the sort of scene they used to talk about all those years ago in London and Paris, confirming Natalie's romantic vision of "ze sous seas". For a moment it has knocked the casual chat out of them.

When we see them next they're off the main road, making their way along a peninsula, Phil doing the map-reading. There are farms and bush and bays and the sea, in altering perspectives and combinations. The road surface changes from tar seal to loose metal. They go through a gate past a notice warning that this is private land and that trespassers will be prosecuted. After another half mile the road peters out. They park the car and go forward on foot.

What they come to finally is a bay, a fine curve of sand with a jetty, and a lone yacht anchored offshore. Big pohutukawas hang over. The land rising from the bay is bush covered. From the jetty they look up into it and shout Jason's name.

No answering shout comes back but there's plenty of evidence of his work. The jetty has new flooring of Australian hardwood, stained red-brown. The bollards are newly painted, white. The piles have new rubber sheathing above the water-line.

They climb the path that goes up from the jetty into the bush. Jason has angled it back and forth across the gradient of the hill, cutting into the bank, making steps, putting down gravel and scoria, driving wooden wedges and in some places steel rods to hold the thick wood, like railway sleepers, he has used to hold his levels in place. Here and there the path takes an unscheduled turn to miss a big tree.

At the top the path brings them out into a clearing. There's a hut with a verandah, the door open and hooked back. Beyond the hut is the space cleared for a house. Already a dozen poles are cemented in place, and there's an arrangement of boards and strings marking floor levels.

From the verandah of the hut they shout Jason's name. Phil manages a two-finger whistle. The sounds echo away over the still bay, but nothing comes back. In the hut everything is in order. Dishes have been done and stacked. The bed is made. The radio is murmuring beside it. The floor has been swept and a rug is hanging over the verandah rail. Some washing is pegged out on a rope stretched between two kauri saplings.

"Fucking Marie Celeste," Phil says. And he goes over and puts his hand on the kettle sitting beside a small stove fed from a gas bottle. The kettle has no heat in it.

So now our shots have to show the passage of time.

Harry sits in a deck chair out on the verandah, drinking a can of beer. A tui sails over the roof and lands with an airy rush on a stalk of flax flowers. It hesitates at the open mouth of a flower, sees Harry watching, and takes off again.

Phil eats a cold sausage out of Jason's kitchen.

Phil stands on the verandah. The sun has moved further to the west. Harry can be seen below the rail urinating in the manuka.

169

Harry pokes around the building site, pacing out the spaces between holes dug to take poles. A wood pigeon creaks over and he looks up, shading his eyes to watch it.

Now they're down on the sand. They strip and swim out to the yacht. It's just a yacht, modest in size, nothing unusual about it. Someone has used it for fishing. Bits of dried bait are stuck to the decking, and fish scales.

Back at the hut they've made themselves tea and they're eating slices of bread.

Now they're out on the verandah, shouting again. Echoes come back. And silence. They stand side by side, listening. There's a sort of breathing through the upper branches of the kauris and a momentary leathery turning of flax blades against one another as a faint breeze gets up from the water. The twittering and flutter of a fantail. Cicadas. Nothing else. No voices. Not even sheep or cows or a dog in the distance.

So our final shots have them closing up the hut and making their way down the path. Half way down, a thin track goes off at an angle, through ferns. Harry turns that way and follows it. It skirts the edge of a steep drop, vertical in places. Twenty feet below, a stream runs. It flows over a drop and settles into a series of deep still pools directly below the track. The pools are calm, and although the stream flows through them, dragging at leaves and reeds, the water is clear. In places the sun angles through it in shafts. In others the surface throws back steely reflections. Harry looks down as into an amphitheatre, roofed over by the canopy of the bush, but broken into here and there by the declining sun.

Now we see Phil stopped on the main path, looking back to see where Harry has gone. He calls.

"Hang on," Harry says. He's crouching now, peering

down. "Phil," he says, and then repeats it because the sound doesn't come out right. "Come and have a look at this."

They crouch side by side, staring down into the still pool twenty feet below.

TWENTY-FOUR

Jason as a Long White Cloud

Harry and Phil were pall-bearers.

It wasn't really a hot day, there was a breeze to cool it, but it was clear and the sun when it struck went straight through your shirt and made itself felt. The sky was blue, but here and there were big lumps of mobile cloud like travelling parasols offering momentary shelter. It was the sort of Auckland light that exposes everything, reveals the mess we've made on a beautiful landscape, and at the same time seems to say Relax! – it doesn't matter. You can tidy up later.

So the body of Jason Cook was borne by his friends out into Dominion Road under that light which penetrates everything and solves no mysteries. Jason was dead, and if God knew how he wasn't saying.

It was like most funerals. There were aunts and uncles and cousins. There were people Jason had worked with. School friends. The groups seemed not to know one another, or even to know of one another's existence. Larson Snow was there, hidden among some men from the trotting fraternity. In a grey suit Larson wasn't instantly recognizable as a plain clothes detective.

Jason's mother lived in a little house in Mt Eden. She'd never lived in Remuera, and it was hard to believe she'd ever drunk sherry. If she owned shares in South African diamond mines they must have been very small shares, and very small diamonds. She was small and thin and her clothes were too big for her, as if she'd been a larger woman who was now fading away. She wore a sky-blue hat that must once have been rather dashing. There was no sign of a husband.

When Mrs Cook shook hands with Harry and Phil she told them she'd heard about them often. Harry wondered what she'd heard and how much of it was true.

They told her what a good friend Jason had been and how much he would be missed.

"He was such a good boy," she said. "Such a very good son."

From a car parked on the opposite side of the street John Sprott took photographs of the mourners. But for what purpose? If there was anything to be known about how Jason had died, those who knew it were hardly likely to attend his funeral.

Harry and Phil stood side by side at the edge of the pavement while Jason's friends and relations murmured greetings and condolences to one another.

"Doesn't seem the right sort of send-off," Harry said.

"How would you do it?"

Harry thought about it. "What about a gondola?"

Phil nodded. After a moment he said, "For some reason I keep thinking of aerial top-dressing."

"You'd have to burn him first."

"Cremate him in a Remuera hedge."

They were standing there staring away from the crowd gathered around the funeral parlour chapel, trying not to look as though they were laughing.

"Thank Christ Jason's not here," Phil said. He was imagining their enigmatic friend as a white cloud streaming out from the tail end of a small plane, spreading and settling over a green landscape.

173

TWENTY-FIVE

Finding the Body

Writing one morning in the café in Rapallo I had got exactly to the point where Harry and Phil crouch side by side looking down at something in the stream, when the phone rang. It was Uta. I was prepared to be angry but her tone of voice disarmed me. She wasn't phoning to reproach me for something I had or hadn't revealed about Harry Butler. She was distressed. The Consul was being recalled to Copenhagen and she had to pack at once and return to Milan. She wondered whether I might spare the time to help her close up the house.

Of course I couldn't refuse – she'd done so much for me. And in any case I didn't want to refuse. I left the blue folder with the padrone and headed off up the salita to Sant' Ambrogio without even returning to the hotel. A light misty rain was falling. A spell of even colder weather was descending over Europe and its edges were reaching down to the Mediterranean.

As I made my way up there I was worried. I felt my work was going steadily forward. But what would be the effect of Uta's departure? I decided my best plan was to keep very calm, to behave as if nothing had happened, and hope the blue folder wouldn't notice her absence.

But there was more to it than that. I'd grown fond of Uta – even dependent on her. I was always complaining to myself about her; but the prospect of her departure seemed to remove from my life in Rapallo one of its few little bits of colour.

There's no need to go into detail. I helped her pack the number two car and lock up the house. She gave me a hundred instructions about what I should do next with the Story, and what I should and shouldn't eat and drink, and how I should keep warm in Rapallo now this January chill was reaching so far south. We kissed one another, first one cheek then the other, southern style, I waved her out of sight, and made my way back down the salita.

Of course the Story wasn't deceived by my attempt to behave as if nothing had changed. It fell silent that same afternoon. "You don't even like her," I said to the silence in my head. "You do nothing but complain about her." Not a word came back. The blue folder lay mute on my hotel bed, declining to argue.

Those days were very dark and lonely. I moved along the coast to Nice, thinking a change of language might help but it didn't. I ate wonderful meals and walked along the seafront, but I knew not a soul, I wasn't working, a depression had settled over Europe and my inner weather matched it exactly. "This has been the worst week of my life," I wrote (exaggerating of course) in a letter home. The next day I took a flight to London.

So I was back where I'd begun, in the little room with the Matisse poster and the Dufy poster and the window overlooking the trees in the square, which had now lost their leaves. Snow was falling, and though it melted on streets and pavements, it lay in the square. What had been green-and-brown was now white-and-black. At least I had friends here, and there were plays to go to, and operas, and concerts, and galleries. I tried to be calm and purposeful. There were revisions to be made, clean copies to be typed.

175

I would sit it out while the Story sulked in its folder.

I credit myself with a certain amount of courage and perseverence. Great qualities – but they did me no good at all. As the days went by and the cold grew more intense, I knew I had to face it. Without Uta there would be no conclusion. Harry Butler would remain where I had last left him, crouching at the edge of the track peering down into a stream destined to flow for ever through that fading afternoon light.

Then one day I arrived back from a gallery to find a message waiting for me, written on a slip of paper by the Cockney woman who cleaned the stairs. Someone called "Hooter" had phoned – and there was a number. I was slow to penetrate this mystery – I was so dulled by the sense of having been defeated. My first thought was that Hooter must be a surname. Or a joke. Then I noticed it wasn't a London number. I dialled the exchange to ask what the area code represented. Of course it was Copenhagen.

I rang at once and "Hooter" answered. She'd tracked me from Rapallo to Nice and from Nice back to London. The Consul had helped, using the services of the Danish diplomatic network. She wanted to know whether I'd finished what she called "our book".

I told her I'd been unable to go on with it in her absence. She was flattered I think, but not surprised. And she mis-understood. She thought I needed her advice and her suggestions and (I suppose) her reproaches. I could hardly tell her it wasn't that at all – it was just that the Story refused to speak. But it didn't matter how much or how little she understood; and I could put up with any amount of her advice, if only I could get working again.

She told me not to worry. She would think of something. She would discuss it with Erik and phone me again tomorrow.

So as the big January freeze of that year iced the roads and burst the waterpipes of Europe, a plan to rescue me was worked out. Uta had for some reason to drive south into Germany, to Kiel. It was decided I should fly to Hamburg, take the train north to Kiel, and she would meet me there and drive me to Copenhagen. Once again she would find me a hotel, though she warned me there would be no cafés in the southern style.

I told her I would work in a telephone booth if necessary, so long as I could be in the same town with her, and see her occasionally. It must have seemed a curiously impassioned statement, and probably she misunderstood it too – though I recognize the possibility that my own understanding of all this was imperfect. At least I knew what I wanted, and Uta was willing to see I got it.

The snow fell and the ice gripped tighter, but I took off on schedule from Heathrow. In Hamburg the little lake in the city centre was frozen and people were walking on it. But I wasted no time there. The bus from the airport took me to the train station, and an hour later I was heading for Kiel through a snow-bound landscape.

Uta met me at the station, we hugged our greeting, and for a moment that incomparable inflation was pressed to my shirt front. In that instant I felt at one with the Story and I knew it would find its voice just as soon as there was a place for me to work.

We were to drive next day to Copenhagen. Meanwhile Uta was staying with some diplomatic people and she'd booked me into a hotel. That night we ate together in a restaurant among fir trees, while outside the snow continued to fall. Uta wanted me to eat something nutritious but I insisted on sausage and sauerkraut and beer. We clanked our pewter mugs together and even banged them on the rough wooden table top, celebrating our reunion and looking forward to the successful completion of our task.

"And now you must tell me at once," she said. "What was it Harry saw down in the stream? It was a body wasn't it?"

I told her it was a body.

"Jason's?"

I nodded again, "Jason's. They weren't quite sure at first. They had to clamber down that steep slope to get a good look at it. It was lying face-up in about three feet of water. It was wedged there between a rock on one side and a water-logged manuka trunk on the other. The water was flowing over and around it – they could see leaves sailing past now and then, across the face. The water was perfectly clear. The face was kind of blown up. Puffy and very white . . ."

Uta shuddered.

"So they were sure it was Jason but they weren't sure, if you know what I mean. And then Phil noticed a hand under the water against that manuka log. It had only four fingers."

Uta shook her head slowly. "Of course. The missing finger on his left hand. So then there was no doubt. It was their friend."

We were silent for a while. Then she asked what they did, what they thought.

"They thought he'd been murdered. And that it had something to do with drugs. It was obvious he was dead. Very dead. So although they went into the water to pull him out, they changed their minds and left him. Phil

178

thought it would be best to get Larson Snow up there straight away. Or at least to let him know what they'd found. So he left Harry beside the stream to watch over the body and he set off running to the car, to find the nearest house with a phone. It seemed the most sensible thing to do. And for a while after Phil left Harry just sat there by the stream, looking down and thinking about Jason."

Uta nodded. "There would be a lot of memories," she said. "And if it was me, a lot of tears too I think."

Again we were silent, imagining Harry sitting there staring down at the beautiful clear cool water, and the brown leaves now and then sailing over the body, maybe hesitating for a moment, clinging to the dead face, and then moving on.

"It would make him think of his old Mind/Body puzzle," Uta said.

"I'm sure it did. Because here was a body without mind. And all around was work that had the particular stamp of Jason Cook. No one else would do things in just that particular way. It's the old story of the millions there are of us and the uniqueness of each one. We want to call it something, so we call it soul. But Harry was back with his old thought. When it's gone it's gone."

Uta looked unseeing for a moment, as if consulting some inner voice for the answer to a problem. Once she had it she came out with it firmly. "I think the soul survives the body," she said.

I shrugged. "I think I'm like Harry."

She laughed at that – I didn't know why. "Of course you are," she said.

We went back to our sausages and sauerkraut. But then I remembered how Harry went on sitting there and the shadows got longer, the sunlight went from the stream, it was still a warm afternoon but there was the sense of a lowering of everything, and suddenly Harry realized he was afraid. In the shock of finding the body they hadn't thought about where the person who'd done this – if there was someone who'd done it – might be.

"I think he was safe," Uta said. "The murderer wouldn't come back. But I would have been scared too. What did Harry do?"

"He stayed there. But he pulled back from the stream. He backed himself into a clump of fern – kept pushing further into it as the light faded. It was very quiet. There was just the sound of tuis calling to one another."

It was almost dark before Phil came back. But when he came it was with a whole team of police including Larson Snow. They had lights, and Larson crouched at the edge of the stream staring down before he gave any instructions. Then John Sprott went to work with his Pentax. The flashes lit up the bush and then it all settled into dark shapes again, until the next flash from a different angle. And they could hear moreporks now, calling and answering. Finally Phil and Harry stood there while two policemen pulled the body out of the water.

Larson Snow was standing just behind them. "If you blokes had some talking to do," he said, "you should have done it to me."

TWENTY-SIX

Babes in the Wood

Larson Snow must have got to the cemetery in the car with John Sprott but he contrived to hitch a lift back into town in the Porsche. Then he suggested a drink, so Harry and Phil found themselves in the Turf Bar with him, where they'd been in the habit of meeting Jason.

"I've started to feel depressed again," Phil said. "What a sod of a thing to happen."

Larson nodded. "You'd known him a long time."

Harry put three beers down on the table. "And you think it was an accident."

"That's what I'm advised," Larson said. "He went down that bank – possibly in the dark – hit his head on a rock so he was unconscious when he went into the water. Not a bad knock, but enough to put him out cold."

"So when he woke up he was dead," Phil said.

"That's more or less the story. Death by drowning."

Harry shook his head. "No one who knew Jason would believe it. He was too competent to fall down that bank and kill himself."

"Funny things happen," Larson said.

Harry shook his head. "Not possible. Not down that bank. Not in that stream."

"So what's the alternative?"

"How about murder," Phil said.

Larson took a sip of his beer. "I know how the idea of murder appeals to you journos."

181

"Go easy," Harry said.

Larson looked unrepentant. "Why didn't you tell me he was a visitor at Greg Carey's?"

Harry and Phil looked at one another.

Larson explained. "John Sprott got half a face along with your shirt-front that morning you turfed us out. It was your pal Jason, wasn't it? Out in Greg Carey's drive."

Harry shrugged. "I didn't see why he should go into drug squad files."

"But you called me when he was dead."

Neither of them had an answer for that.

"And now you're suggesting he might have been murdered."

"You must have thought of that yourself," Phil said.

"I've thought of it. I haven't found any reasons for believing it."

"But you must have looked into what he was doing up there on the peninsula. Who owns the land. Who was employing him."

Larson nodded. "I've done that. Sure."

"And you're not going to tell us."

Larson was silent a moment. He lit a cigarette. "He was employed by the owners of the land. It's owned by a company."

Phil laughed. "I bet it is."

The fifth race from Ellerslie was broadcast over the sound-system. Larson listened to it, sipping his beer. When it was over he made a little note on the back of his cigarette packet. As he put it into his pocket he said to Harry, "Did Phil tell you I have a theory about you and Mandy Rivers?"

Harry looked at Phil.

"I told him," Phil said.

182

"So what d'you say? Was it a good theory?"

"I met her in Singapore," Harry said. "You were right about that."

"And you told her we were watching her house."

Harry was leaning forward, elbows on knees, staring at the ground between his feet. "An impulse, I'm afraid."

Larson shook his head and whistled quietly. "Intellectuals," he said. "Fucking babes in the wood."

"Where is she now," Phil asked.

"Gone. We've lost the trail. That probably means she and Greg Carey are back in Australia. They could be picked up over there for drug offences, but if they run true to form we probably won't hear of them again for two or three years. When we do it might be because they're dead."

"This company," Phil said. "The one that owns the land."

"Five shareholders," Larson said.

"One holds 98 per cent of the shares," Phil said. "And he's a lawyer. Right?"

"We're all good at guessing today," Larson said.

"I think Jason went to Greg Carey's place to get payment for the work he was doing. If that's right, it links drugs with that property he was working on. All you have to imagine is a drug drop offshore – from a big yacht to a smaller one before the big one gets to port."

"I do know how it's done, pal," Larson said.

"It's the ideal place for it."

"It's a nice place for a holiday home too, and that's what they say they're building up there. Now the nest's been fouled that's probably what it will be."

"How do you explain Jason's visit to Greg Carey's house?"

"Officially I don't have to explain it. I don't know about it, because your mate here shoved his shirt in front of our camera."

"But you do know about it," Phil said.

Larson Snow stared back. "Ever thought he might have been there as a customer? Carey didn't only sell heroin. What about cocaine? Or just some very good imported hash? If I look into that visit, that's the line I'll be taking."

They were silent again. Larson seemed to soften a little. "What you have to understand," he said, "is that the drug landscape's littered with corpses. Not pretty ones, most of them. Even if I did believe your mate was murdered, there's nothing I could do about it. No evidence. Nothing to go on. So until you've got something better to offer me it's going to have to stay just as it is. An accident. That way's better for our statistics."

TWENTY-SEVEN

Uta Makes War on a Cliché

When Uta and I came out of the restaurant the snow had made rounded heaps on the stone steps and frozen solid, with a moist slippery surface impossible to walk on. We had to lower ourselves down, clinging with both hands to the verandah rail. Then the car skidded on the cobbled streets, and when I got out to push, my feet slid away under me. Somehow Uta got me to my hotel; and ten minutes later, as arranged, she phoned to say she'd reached her friends" house safely. I slept naked in the warm hotel room under one of those German feather quilts, sweating, and dreaming of a body under water that smiled and spoke to me but I couldn't hear what it was saying.

Next day the snow was falling again but the temperature had risen. Uta arrived soon after I'd eaten my breakfast. The snow ploughs had been out and she wanted us to get as far as we could before the freeze began once more. If she didn't get back to Copenhagen that evening Erik would worry. And it would be inconvenient. I can't say I worried for myself. The thought of spending a night with Uta somewhere along the way appealed to me, and I was pretty sure it would please the Story too.

But we made good time. At Flensburg we crossed the border into Denmark and drove on up the Jutland peninsula. There were glimpses of a frozen river and a frozen shore-line. The snow showers came and went but the road stayed open, and by the time we stopped for lunch Uta was sure we were going to get through. She hadn't taken the most direct route but the one Erik thought most likely to stay open and get us there safely.

So we crossed by bridge to the island of Fyn and continued east towards Nyborg where with luck there would be a ferry to Sjaelland and the road to Copenhagen.

It must have been somewhere along the road to Nyborg that Uta told me, in that tone of hers which suggested her word on certain matters was beyond question, that I would have to make some changes in the scene in which two radical feminists in overalls visit Louise Lamont. Why were they both short, she wanted to know. (I'd noticed that Uta tended to frown on shortness, as if it was a sign of failure.) And why did one have to be fat? And why both in overalls with short-cropped hair? She said it wasn't fair. If I hadn't said all Harry Butler's women were beautiful I'd certainly implied it. And then when a couple of radical feminists came on the scene they had to be presented as ugly.

"I didn't say they were ugly," I protested.

"Well . . ." Uta waved a free hand. "Short. Spiky-haired, fat, overalls – we all know the type."

I asked her why she was complaining if she knew the type.

"Because . . ." she hesitated. "I suppose because not all feminists are like that."

"But a lot are," I said. "And it happens that these ones were. I'm sticking to the facts."

Uta thought there were times when I might have to depart from the facts to avoid a cliché. To avoid appearing prejudiced.

"As it happens," I said, "I am prejudiced. But so are

186

you. After all, what's wrong with overalls and spiky hair? They wouldn't like what you wear. They'd say you were a slave to fashion."

"You didn't have to call them dykes," she said.

I pointed out that it was Louise Lamont who called them dykes. "You're the one who's prejudiced," I told her. "They call themselves dykes. They're proud of it. Les used to wear a badge sometimes that said DYKE."

"But you implied they stole Harry Butler's letter to Louise."

"They did steal it."

Uta shook her head. We were bowling along a motorway cleared of snow. The snow was piled on either side and heaped against fences built to stop it drifting. "Hasn't it occurred to you," she said, "that they wanted to help Louise? Didn't she need help? Maybe she should have listened to them."

"I don't think they wanted to help her," I said. "They wanted to harm Harry. They said he was guilty of sexual harassment and he had to be punished. They even said he was a rapist."

"Well . . ." Uta shrugged. "Maybe in their terms he was."

"Oh great," I said. "When the Brigata Rossa blows up Erik and says he was a tool of international capitalism I'll remember to quote you."

We did a swerve in the road. I thought we must have run into ice until I saw it was the shock effect of what I'd said.

"I'm sorry Uta," I said. "That was thoughtless."

We drove on in silence until we came to Nyborg and the ferry.

The excitement of the crossing restored our spirits. The

187

sea was frozen but the surface was cracked into great fragments which broke with a continuous graunching and grinding noise as the ship ploughed through. All around there was grey fog, and below the window at which Uta and I sat drinking strong coffee and eating sandwiches the grey-white surface of the ice was broken and heaved aside by the shuddering hull.

We were both lit up by the drama of it, and when the ice was especially thick so the ferry, breaking through, shuddered from end to end and seemed to hesitate as if it might lose heart, Uta grabbed my hand on the table top and squeezed tight. As if to encourage herself she told me that when the Danes were fighting the Germans in the year 1219, and losing, the heavens opened and a flag fell to earth. The Danes took it up, fought with redoubled strength, and won. Thereafter that was the Danish flag.

So the ferry berthed, we drove the car out of the hold, and now the road to Copenhagen lay ahead of us. I offered to drive, but Uta didn't feel sure someone from "ze sous seas" would recognize the signs if the road began to freeze.

"I hope you know what you're doing," she said. "That sea we've just crossed will be frozen hard by tomorrow. If the airports close, you've locked yourself in."

I said I'd thought you could cross from Copenhagen to Sweden.

She shook her head. "The hydrofoils stopped days ago. It's frozen on that side too."

"Well," I shrugged. "I wasn't planning to go anywhere. And if I change my mind, I'll walk."

Shortly after that I drifted off to sleep. When I woke I had my head on Uta's shoulder and we were just coming out of a misty white landscape into the suburbs of Copenhagen.

The Comfort Hotel in which she'd booked me was close to the Town Hall. I could see its brown tower and gold-faced clock and hear its chimes from my room. There was a table at the window and a chair.

"You might have to work here," Uta said. "A café of the kind you like will be hard to find."

I'd taken the blue folder out of my luggage and thrown it on the bed. I knew I was going to be able to continue, and I felt a surge of gratitude.

Uta was standing with her back to the window, half sitting on the edge of the desk. "Is it satisfactory," she asked.

"It's perfect," I hadn't overcome my fear of her, but the impulse drove through it. I said: "I want to kiss you."

She closed her eyes. "Hurry," she said.

I was confused by that. Hurry? It checked my forward movement. I kissed her on the mouth, but only a sort of momentary pressure and then I drew back.

She opened her eyes. "Is that all?"

Then I kissed her properly.

She liked it, but in a moment she'd regained her composure. Somehow she got herself past me, and out the door. Before closing it she said, "Work now. Don't waste time. I'll see if they will bring up coffee for you."

TWENTY-EIGHT

Thinking with the Body

It was a day or so after the funeral that Les and Midge
struck. When Harry got to his office he found Edith in
tears. She didn't seem able to explain to him what was
wrong, although she tried. It was one of his senior colleagues who took him aside and told him the shit had hit
the fan.

Scattered all over the university, pinned to notice-
boards, left on desks in lecture rooms and the library, and
on tables in the student union cafeteria, there were xeroxed
copies of two extracts carefully selected from Harry's
letter to Louise, unmistakably in his handwriting, and
each with a printed message underneath.

The first read:

> Did I tell you about my dream? We were fucking in an
> inflatable dinghy. Then we looked up and saw we'd
> drifted into the library. It was a bit like Venice, with
> canals and bridges. The Dean was looking down from
> the mezzanine floor, pointing and shouting that Harry
> Butler was "doing it" with a student. Even in the dream
> it seemed funny that he said "doing it".

The note printed underneath this extract read

DO YOU WANT TO FIGURE IN HARRY BUTLER'S DREAM
LANDSCAPE? OR DO YOU THINK PROFESSORS WHO HARASS

THEIR STUDENTS SEXUALLY SHOULD BE SACKED? WOMEN:
MAKE YOUR FEELINGS KNOWN!

And the second extract:

> I remember the first time you came to my office. You
> said you were having problems with the Symbolic
> Logic paper, but all the signals were telling me some-
> thing else. I suppose I should have told you not to come
> back, but even now I can't feel any guilt about it. It
> happened, that's all – to me as much as to you. And
> once it had happened I didn't feel "older", or the pro-
> fessor, any longer. All of that was wiped out.

And the accompanying message:

HOW WOULD YOU FEEL ABOUT TAKING A PROBLEM TO THE
PROFESSOR WHO WROTE THIS TO A WOMAN STUDENT? HIS
NAME IS HARRY BUTLER. WOMEN: TELL THE UNIVERSITY
WHERE YOU THINK HE SHOULD GO!

Harry withdrew into his room and shut the door, having
told Edith to stop sniffing and that he wouldn't be available to anyone. He could guess what was going on. All
around the university there would be excitement, some
joking, moral indignation in some quarters, anxiety in
others, and everyone speculating about whether this
meant Harry Butler was on the skids. No doubt the Vice
Chancellor would welcome a resignation and a quiet
departure. The Dean might be pleased (Harry had still not
supplied the information the Dean needed about the new
building). In Womenspace over at the student union there
might be anything from quiet satisfaction to a noisy
celebration.

Harry sat with copies of the xeroxes scattered over his

desk trying to discover what it was he felt. An unusual stillness had settled over him.

There had been rain in the night – a warm north-easterly blowing the far edges of a tropical storm in from the Pacific. The palm heads were tossing in it, the harbour was pale blue and white, and the gulls had allowed themselves to be flung ashore for a casual meeting around the water-metal fountain. Everywhere the air moved in spasms, unpredictably, making itself felt; but at the same time it was mild.

Harry went to the window and stood looking down watching the tossed gulls going with the gusts. Whoever had circulated the extracts had protected Louise. She wasn't identified. They must have had the letter from her. But Harry stuck on that point. He couldn't imagine Louise doing such a thing, even in anger.

He couldn't understand his own calm. He felt at home in his body and his body was relaxed. He moved his shoulders experimentally, lifting them and pushing them forward. It was as if he was thinking with his body. If he was about to lose his job it might be as well. Already the job had lost him.

He went to his desk and began to set out all the facts the Dean needed for the Philosophy Department's share of the new building. He had them on separate sheets of paper in a clip. One by one he transcribed the pieces of information until a picture of the Department's needs began to emerge.

He worked for some hours. Once Edith tapped and told him there had been a call from the Vice Chancellor's office. He was wanted over there. Harry nodded but he ignored it. He made himself a cup of coffee and went on working.

That afternoon he climbed the path through trees, up

from Grafton Road into the Domain. The wind had almost gone, the sun had come out, the air was damp and warm and heavy. The trees were loud with cicadas. The late sunlight seemed magnified, as if by the glass of moisture through which it was passing.

The Porsche when he got to it was a moderate oven. As soon as he got behind the wheel he broke out in a sweat. He drove along Shore Road, up Ngapipi Road, down towards Mission Bay, wondering why he had ever wanted such a car. His comfortable, well-appointed, high-status, up-market, purgatorial chariot. With ski-racks. With everything.

Along Arvon Crescent he passed Jonah and Reuben playing under the trees. They had a Tarzan rope on which they swung out over a bank. They waved and shouted as the Porsche cruised around the curve of the street. Harry waved back and sounded the horn.

He put the car away and went around the side of the house, stopping to see how the grape clusters were developing. There was no sound coming from the kitchen. He went in. On the kitchen table an envelope addressed to Claire Butler was torn open. His letter to Louise Lamont was on the floor. Not a copy. The whole thing.

Harry called. There was no reply. He listened. He could hear a faint murmuring, and as he got nearer to the room that had once been his study it grew more distinct.

In there Claire was once again at the shrine among flowers, rocking gently backwards and forwards watched by the clay figure of the whirling dervish, chanting "I am not this body I am not this body I am not this body I am not this body . . ."

"Claire."

He spoke her name tentatively and she took no notice.

She was perhaps so far lost in her mantra that she didn't hear. Or maybe she was just ignoring him.

He tried again but she didn't stop. He watched her for a moment and then went away in the direction of the bedroom.

Harry took a suitcase from the cupboard above the wardrobe and began packing.

TWENTY-NINE

Hurry and Hooter

I was working now in a brown city locked in a white circle. I ate my breakfast, and sometimes other meals too, in a little red and black restaurant with frilly light shades that hung over the tables. I sat at a desk in my room, and when I looked up I could see ice sliding almost imperceptibly down the red-tiled roof opposite. Now and then a piece would break off and fall over people walking in the street below. Beyond that roof the brown tower and the gold-faced clock pushed up into the cold haze of the sky.

Not far away the Tivoli Gardens were closed. When I walked that way I could see through the iron gate the elegant black curves of willows hanging over frozen ponds.

In the afternoons I walked along frozen canals and down to the frozen docks. Sometimes I went as far as the harbour where the little mermaid sat on her rock, surrounded by ice. I stared across the ice towards Sweden, but everything out there vanished in a haze.

Uta came and went, checking drafts, proof-reading clean copies of early chapters. After that kiss on the day of arriving I played a game of cat and mouse with her. I think she enjoyed it, so long as she made the rules and the rules ensured that she always won. I would walk out to the car with her. Snow was usually falling, or about to fall, or had just fallen.

"Go back inside," she said. "You'll catch cold."

"I want to kiss you."

She looked up and down the street. It was empty. "Not here," she said. "Not in the street."

I stood my ground. She stepped back into a doorway, pulling me after her by the lapels. "Hurry," she said.

So I kissed her, and she drove away with another bundle of typescript.

When she came to the hotel she rang from downstairs. I always invited her up to my room, but she never came. She would wait for me down in the little black and red restaurant. Often she read things while I had my breakfast.

Then one day there was a knock at my door. I went. It was Uta with a few pages of typescript in her hand. I stood back and she walked in. She looked different – possibly upset.

"You keep your room tidy," she said approvingly.

She went over to the window and looked out. Big flakes were streaming past the window, too heavy to be disturbed by any upward draft of air.

I'm not sure I can recall the exact sequence in which things were said, but I know that at some point she looked at me and said "Hurry". I'd made no move in her direction, but I took this as a kind of signal. After all, this was the first time since installing me that she'd come to my room. I moved towards her, but she turned her head away.

I was confused. "Why do you tell me to hurry," I said.

"Not hurry," she said. "*Harry*."

And then she began to talk about the sheets of typescript she'd brought with her. The two things went together in my mind. I was listening to what she was saying. And at the same time I was working out just what it meant that she called me Harry.

196

I couldn't tell when it had begun but I saw now that at some point she must have got hold of the idea that I was Harry Butler telling his own story. Of course she knew that names would have been changed and identities concealed; but allowing for that, she saw the story as a piece of disguised autobiography. That explained why at times her anger with me and with the character of Harry had been so difficult to disentangle; and maybe also why as Harry's fortunes had declined, she'd softened towards me.

Now she'd got hold of those pages in which the extracts of Harry's letter are circulated around the university, and he goes home to find Claire back at her shrine. That must have confirmed me as Harry. Claire had retreated into the world of the Sufi, I had lost my job, packed my bag, and come abroad to write my story – and she, Uta Haverstrom, was helping me.

It was an ending – even a tragic one. But though it made her sorry for "Hurry", it also made her impatient with him. More important, it altered her attitude to Claire. How could Claire have retreated like that in such a crisis? What sort of a woman was she? Where was her courage and her feminine resourcefulness? How could she be party to a weak ending?

I felt cowed by this onslaught. My hopes had been high when Uta's sweater had presented itself at my door.

"I'm not Harry," I said.

Uta looked at me for a moment. "Are you sure?"

As soon as I'd said it I thought I might have made a mistake. Even if she didn't like what she called a weak ending, her pity for "Hurry", defeated at home and driven abroad to tell his story, might have been the very means to changing the rules of our game. But it was too late now.

197

"Quite sure," I said.

"Then who are you," she asked. "How do you know so much?"

THIRTY

In and Out of Harry's Suitcase

So here I am back in my room in London where I began, looking out over winter trees. There has been a thaw. The view is no longer black and white but a sort of dirty grey. I can feel it – the time for me to return to "ze sous seas" is approaching. The brown city locked in a white circle has released me, and now the raven on the sill, as in "Edgar Allenbow" and Paul Gaugin, is "quothing" *Nevermore*! In my end is my beginning.

No I am not Harry Butler come abroad to write his memoirs. I am (let's say) unpaid secretary to the Story. And though some frozen land-and-seascapes now lie between me and the Great Dane, the blue folder hasn't fallen silent. Not yet. Not quite.

Was the outcome which Uta imagined to be the end an unhappy one? Obviously she thought so. It made her sorry for Harry and angry with Claire. It also left her dissatisifed. She might have condemned the way I'd presented Midge and Les, but now she wanted to know why they should be allowed the victory. It would take (she said) more than overalls and spiky hairstyles to overturn a million years of biological history. Uta was fierce. I'd often wondered how it was that Europeans, these grey, unphysical creatures, had conquered the world. With Uta there could be no such puzzle. In her eyes at that moment I saw bearskins and horned helmets and fires on the ice.

But it's the story's end that concerns me. What Uta that morning imagined it to be she called a tragedy. I don't think she meant a noble tragedy, as in Shakespeare: I think she meant something regrettable that shouldn't have been allowed to happen – and I suppose that's true. An end to those moments of intuition and accord, where Claire's hand on Harry's or his on hers, and the right word casually exchanged, took them right back to the passion of that moment on the wooden verandah where it began. A severance of Harry from Jonah and Reuben on their Tarzan rope, or in the sailboat he was to buy them for the summer. A finish to an academic career and to the reputation, mobility and affluence that went with it.

But that was not the end, and when you know it was not, your feelings – a man's feelings, or perhaps I should simply say mine – are likely to be less clear. Undisciplined thinking was one of the charges levelled at Harry Butler – rather like the charge of "conduct unbecoming to an officer". As a philosopher he was considered to have become imprecise, tending to the grandiose. To some of his friends and some of his students what that meant was that he'd become interesting. The hitherto limpid and impeccable stream of his thought was now prone (especially during those Thursday seminars) to flash floods.

I'm sorry if this sounds obscure. What is going around in my head, as I take down the Matisse poster and roll it into a cardboard tube for sending home, is simply a question: if Harry had been sacked, disgraced, and sent forth (as we say) naked into the world, would it have been all bad? Might he not have discovered himself, in action and in thought, and in the thought that springs from action? But in this I suppose I'm revealing only my incurably romantic soul, or turning autobiographical, rather than doing my job which is to set down what happened.

When Claire Butler retired to her shrine and chanted her favourite mantra she was not, as Harry thought, withdrawing from him once again, and finally, into the world of the Sufi. She was merely gathering strength. Before his suitcase was half full she'd emerged from the shrine and was issuing orders with the calm confidence of a field commander on the eve of battle. At that moment Harry was in no mood to argue. To be directed was what he craved. The underpants and socks went back into the drawer, the shirts went back on their hangers, and Harry went off in the Porsche to the nearest Chinese restaurant to buy vegetarian takeaways while Claire got to work on the phone.

I've described the strange calm that settled over Harry when he heard about the xeroxes. It was something that seemed to express itself physically. He was at ease with his own body, and because of that it seemed to him he was ready to face whatever consequences there had to be. But that was something he could preserve only in his office with the door closed, or walking home through the trees of the Domain. Probably it began to be lost when he climbed into his car. It was, after all, parked in the sun every day; but that day the sweat broke out on his brow as soon as he got in behind the wheel.

Then there was the moment of seeing Jonah and Reuben on their Tarzan rope. As they waved and shouted he felt a terrifying lurch in the stomach.

During that afternoon, working steadily through his clip of the Department's needs to compile a submission for the Dean, Harry was aware that he would have to tell Claire what had happened. Probably she'd already guessed that he was having an affair with Louise. In any case there would be no hiding it now. He would have to work that out – how it was to be done – but meanwhile that problem too was pushed to the back of his mind. He worked on steadily with the top of his consciousness, while somewhere deeper there was the sense of having settled into himself, of knowing who he was and what he required of himself. But how secure was he in that?

Not very, we have to suppose; because the discovery that Claire had already been told, and in the most brutal way – his own letter lying there on the kitchen floor, while Claire seemed to have retreated once more into her Sufi mantra – this destroyed at once and completely what in any case I don't suppose could have lasted. Now he was indeed at war with himself. The stomach tightening, pulse racing, breath catching, pressure behind the eyes – all the signs were there. And when he went to pack his suitcase, it was not with calm resolve, the strong man going forth. It was in the spirit of a man defeated and retreating. He felt as if his legs might buckle. His arms didn't work properly and his fingers failed in the simple action of folding a shirt. So when Claire emerged from her chanting and told him to put his clothes back where they belonged and not to be melodramatic, Harry didn't hesitate, even for a moment. A great surge of relief, and of gratitude, washed over him.

THIRTY-ONE

The Death of the Body

Now we really have need of the camera team. How else can we deal with Claire in action? We have to see her talking to Harry, to Louise, to the Vice Chancellor or Chancellor, maybe also to the student President or the editor of the student newspaper. Queen Claire. Claire victorious.

And there's something odd in these scenes. Have we described Claire? Wasn't she depicted as small? She can't have grown, but now she has taken on something of the Uta look – tall, Nordic, blonde, blue-eyed, with even, it seems, some perceptible enlargement of the bust.

Harry believed there was nothing to be done. Alone in his room that afternoon, putting together his submission to the Dean in the spirit of a man setting his house in order before leaving it, Harry prided himself on being ready to confront the truth and acknowledge it. Images of his breast bravely bared to the knife, or his collar removed to facilitate the executioner's axe, may not have been present to his consciousness but they wouldn't have been totally alien to the spirit in which he looked to the future. When you can't live, you can at least die nobly. Harry was ready to say in effect, "Yes, this is the kind of man I am, and the kind of life I've lived. It's up to you what you do about it."

"How boring," says Claire. "How uninventive. There's always an alternative."

"What's the alternative to the truth," Harry wants to know.

"The alternative," Claire tells him, "is the big flat lie. The real whopper."

"But the letter . . ." Harry begins.

"I have it," Claire says. "They sent it to me."

"But they've circulated extracts," Harry points out.

"Of a letter you wrote to a student," Claire says. "Have you forgotten I was your student ten years ago? There's nothing in those extracts that you couldn't have written to me. And the person who received it isn't named."

"It seems too risky," Harry says. "What if it doesn't work?"

"If it doesn't work we're no worse off. It just means I tried to save you and I failed."

At the door she turns, pushing a strand of blond hair back from her blue eyes. "But I don't intend to fail," she says.

So we see Claire next with Louise. They may be talking across a table on that very terrace where we began, outside the Auckland Art Gallery. Why should our lens not zoom in, as before, from the slopes of the park? Louise's Italian shoes haven't worn well, but never mind. She's not going to rub Claire's calf with them. And there's no glass prism on the table between them to catch the light and distract us.

They like one another well enough. At least they find it possible to talk civilly. Two women, Midge and Les, have upset the social order; now two others, Claire and Louise, are going to restore it. All Claire needs of Louise is a promise that if she's asked she will deny ever having received a letter from Harry. Louise promises willingly enough. She's angry at the theft of the letter; angrier at the use that has been made of it. And even if she felt differently about it, she doesn't want to be at the centre of a scandal.

"Hold to that," Claire says, "and don't let anyone shake you. But if things work out as I think they will, you won't even be asked the question."

"Aren't you underestimating those two," Louise says.

"Midge and Les? Aren't you forgetting they acted anonymously? They can't come out of the woodwork and argue about it without admitting they did it."

Now Claire is in the university's most spacious and well-appointed office, ushered in by an anxious secretary. She sits in a huge leather chair which fails to diminish her, and stares blue-eyed across a broad polished desk, quite empty of papers, at an elderly and senior officer of the institution – possibly even the Chancellor himself – a retired judge of the High Court, a knighted surgeon, a general perhaps, someone used to issuing orders calmly under fire.

Claire has declined tea and coffee. She has come straight to the point. A letter written to her by her husband ten years ago has been stolen and extracts circulated around the university. Claire lets the venerable bigwig know she's upset (anger is signified, not tears). This can't be waved away as an average student prank. Its intentions are malicious and its effects damaging. Claire holds the Chancellor and the University Council responsible. She will be consulting her lawyer.

Her message to the officers of the Student Union is the same, though she puts it across less legalistically, with a little more pathos but not too much. She cares about this invasion of her privacy. She cares about the malicious use that has been made of the letter. And she mourns the loss of the letter itself, which was something she valued – no, not valued. In our script she might go so far as to say it was something she *treasured*.

Now the rumour – something we can't focus our cameras on – is spreading through the university community. Did you know . . .? Have you heard . . .? Everyone wants to be first with the latest. Harry Butler's private letter to a student was really . . .

Some people find it hard to believe. But then (others argue) why, if it's not true, would the wronged wife say so? There are some hardliners who say it doesn't matter whether the letter was written this year or ten years ago, it's still evidence of unacceptable behaviour and wrong attitudes to a woman student. But you can feel the tension going out of it. What was a scandal is turning into a joke, or at worst, an embarrassment.

Maybe our last shot in this sequence should be of Harry. Claire has won. Harry is back in his office, staring at his desk – perfectly tidy as he left it – everything in order. Now he must be recognizing how completely that last afternoon was devoted to putting his things straight before leaving them behind for ever. There's even a list of his remaining lectures for the term, and suggestions as to who should give them. His unmarked essays are divided according to topic, with the names of colleagues who should mark them attached. A suicide note is all it would have needed to set the seal and express the mood which Claire dismissed as melodrama.

What is that look in Harry's eye as he stands staring down at his desk? It's certainly not triumph. But not despair either. It's something so neutral it's hard to be sure what it is. Probably just acceptance, as a well-trained dog accepts when you chain it to its kennel for the night. It is, after all, quite a long chain, and an unusually well-appointed kennel.

But to be quite fair and honest, it has to be admitted that the image of the dog doesn't do justice to Harry. Dogs don't smile; or if, as dog-lovers assert, they do, they don't smile *wryly*. Usually they grin and pant and thump the floor with their tails – or they howl at the moon; in between those extremes of emotion there are not a lot of subtle shades. Harry isn't thumping as he looks down at his desk, but he isn't howling either.

From now on that door between Harry and Edith will remain more or less permanently ajar. His Thursday seminars will take on a more structured character. He will become a more disciplined academic, a more compliant husband, a more dutiful father, a more dependable person. He will even patch up his differences with the Dean. Harry has come to heel.

Yes, it's acceptance, and yes, it's wry. Is it also the death of the body? Who can say?

THIRTY-TWO

What is the Purpose of Your Visit?

Uta (to go back a couple of days) was delighted with the new ending – the real ending, as she called it; and now the northern weather, which seemed to have acted in collaboration with her, was easing its grip. The fogs lifted and the white circle around the brown city began to break up. The calendar and my bank balance told me I had already overstayed. As soon as I was able I booked a seat for London.

Uta came to my room that morning. She helped me pack. There were still bits and pieces in rough draft and we went down to the red and black restaurant, ordered coffee, and began to go over them. Uta had made some notes for me so I wouldn't make mistakes putting the typescript together finally in London.

"Remember you still have to say what happened to Louise," she said.

I nodded. "I won't forget."

"Do you want to go over it with me?"

"Well . . ." There was no need, but we had time to spare. "Louise lived most of a year with Matthew," I said. "Then she left him to take up a scholarship at Berkeley in California."

Uta nodded approvingly. "So she never saw Harry again."

"She saw him. He didn't see her. Louise was on a flying

visit to Auckland. She decided to call in at the university and say hullo. In the Department office she got the ice-water treatment from Edith. But she managed to get out of her that Harry had just left to give a lecture. Louise went after him. She caught up with him waiting to cross a street on his way to a lecture theatre. He looked pretty tense . . ."

Uta interrupted. "In what way tense?"

"Shoulders hunched up. Talking to himself."

"Going over points he wanted to make in his lecture," Uta said.

"Probably. And he looked smaller than Louise remembered him."

"Smaller?" Uta didn't like the sound of that. "What is all this meant to suggest?"

"I think it shows Louise recognizing at last that for her it was all over. Harry wasn't any longer a romantic figure. So she just let him go. He hadn't seen her and she decided what was in the past was better left there."

Uta nodded and made a tick at the bottom of the page of notes. Our coffee was brought and she made the old joke about Balzac. That reminded us of the padrone in Milan. "When you get back there," I said, "you must tell him the job's done, and give him my salutes."

Uta looked again at her notebook. "And Harry became a better philosopher," she said.

"His colleagues said so," I confirmed. "He reoccupied the little room at home – the one that had been Claire's shrine. But his interests shifted. He gave up the old Mind/Body conundrum."

"It was time for a change," Uta said.

"He began to work on Wittgenstein. In fact just that day of Louise's visit he got word that a paper called 'Colour: a

Late Wittgenstein Crux' had been accepted by the *Philosophical Quarterly*."

Uta nodded. "Good. And Claire – she didn't mind giving him back the room?"

I explained that Claire hadn't renounced her Sufism, but that her interests, too, were shifting. She no longer attended Duag MacPherson's sessions. In fact she was doing some post-graduate courses at the university, including one in Harry's Department.

"And the boys – Jonah and Reuben?"

"They're fine," I told her. "They got their sailboat. You can see them most afternoons through the summer down on the bay."

Uta drove me to the airport. I checked in my luggage and we waited for my call. Uta told me Erik sent his regards. "And I have something for you," she said.

She handed me a small present, neatly wrapped in paper decorated with the Dannebrog. I shook it, sniffed it, weighed it in my hand, but I couldn't guess what it was. So I unwrapped it. It was a small black compass with red lettering. "It points north, you see," Uta said.

"Hooter," I said. And I kissed her on the cheek.

"Hurry," she replied, and kissed me on the mouth.

My first boarding call had come before she remembered the last thing she'd meant to ask. What had become of Phil?

"He went on working for his paper," I told her. "He spent a lot of time trying to solve the mystery of Jason Cook's death. Sometimes he thought he had a promising lead, but it never brought him to anything like a firm conclusion. In the end he gave it up and decided to turn what he knew about it into a book. He took leave from his paper for a few months and went abroad to work on it. He meant it to be a kind of thriller, but in the course of writing it turned into something different."

My second call came over the loud speaker.

Uta was silent, holding on to my lapels as she'd done in the street outside the Comfort Hotel, staring at me as if she didn't know what to believe.

"Time to go," I said.

We hugged one another silently. A few minutes later I was settling into my seat, fastening my seatbelt.

To get an early flight I'd had to book Club Class. It meant free drinks and a good meal. For the latter half of the flight I sank into one of those dozes in which what you experience is a dream except that you retain some control over it. It was built around that moment in the Comfort Hotel when I told Uta that I wasn't "Hurry". I saw a whole alternative sequence of events in which I confirmed her belief that I was Harry Butler writing concealed autobiography, and she, taking pity on the man who had been rejected, sacked, and sent packing in this darkest hour, offered the consolation of that splendid bosom and everything that went along with it. As the dream developed I recognized how different an outcome that would have been. There might have been no conclusion to our book. I had lost Uta almost by the accident of the wrong answer at the wrong moment. By the same accident I suppose the Story had survived.

Dreams like that can only be sustained at an altitude of 35,000 feet. At Heathrow, while former SS officers and Luftwaffe pilots walked through unchallenged on their EC passports, I was held up, along with other British Commonwealth aliens, to be asked, as always, "What is the purpose of your visit?" It's a difficult moment. What, after all, would you do if, arriving at the door of your favourite aunt, you were greeted with that question? I'd tried "The visit is the purpose" as an answer when flying in last from Nice. It was the truth, but it hadn't helped me get through quickly.

"Whart is the porpoise of yorr wisit," asked the Sikh immigration officer. Indians were always the hardest to get past. Having once got through the barrier themselves they tended to guard it with the zeal of a mad dog. I remembered the lesson I'd learned in the Comfort Hotel. The truth may not always get you what you want.

"I'm attending a conference on ethnic minorities," I told him.

The power of fiction was exemplified in the speed with which his stamp came down on my passport.

That same evening I sorted my papers on the desk over-looking the square. Everything seemed in order. Everything accounted for. Then I remembered one small item I'd omitted. I phoned through a telegram to go to Uta. It read:

GREG CAREY FOUND DEAD IN SYDNEY STOP LARSON SNOW HAS UNCONFIRMED REPORT THAT MANDY NOW WORKING AS SINGER IN HONG KONG NIGHTCLUB